SENTIMENTAL TALES

RUSSIAN LIBRARY

R

The Russian Library at Columbia University Press publishes an expansive selection of Russian literature in English translation, concentrating on works previously unavailable in English and those ripe for new translations. Works of premodern, modern, and contemporary literature are featured, including recent writing. The series seeks to demonstrate the breadth, surprising variety, and global importance of the Russian literary tradition and includes not only novels but also short stories, plays, poetry, memoirs, creative nonfiction, and works of mixed or fluid genre.

■ □ ■

Between Dog and Wolf by Sasha Sokolov, translated by Alexander Boguslawski
Strolls with Pushkin by Andrei Sinyavsky, translated by Catharine Theimer
  Nepomnyashchy and Slava I. Yastremski
Fourteen Little Red Huts and Other Plays by Andrei Platonov, translated
  by Robert Chandler, Jesse Irwin, and Susan Larsen
Rapture: A Novel by Iliazd, translated by Thomas J. Kitson
City Folk and Country Folk by Sofia Khvoshchinskaya, translated
  by Nora Seligman Favorov
Writings from the Golden Age of Russian Poetry by Konstantin Batyushkov,
  presented and translated by Peter France
Found Life: Poems, Stories, Comics, a Play, and an Interview by Linor Goralik,
  edited by Ainsley Morse, Maria Vassileva, and Maya Vinokur
Sisters of the Cross by Alexei Remizov, translated by Roger John Keys
  and Brian Murphy

MIKHAIL ZOSHCHENKO

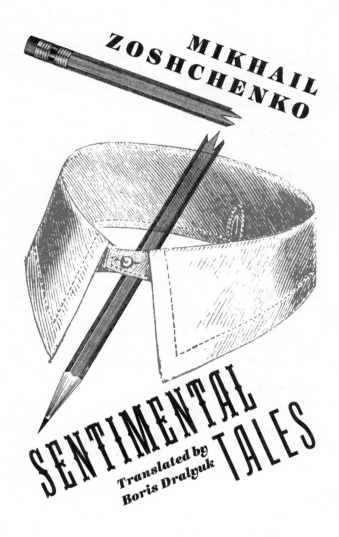

SENTIMENTAL TALES

Translated by
Boris Dralyuk

Columbia University Press / New York

Published with the support of Read Russia, Inc., and the Institute of
     Literary Translation, Russia
Columbia University Press
Publishers Since 1893
New York   Chichester, West Sussex
cup.columbia.edu

Cataloging-in-Publication Data available from the Library of Congress

ISBN 978-0-231-18378-9 (cloth)
ISBN 978-0-231-18379-6 (paper)
ISBN 978-0-231-54515-0 (electronic)

Columbia University Press books are printed on permanent
     and durable acid-free paper.
Printed in the United States of America

Cover design: Roberto de Vicq de Cumptich
Book design: Lisa Hamm

CONTENTS

ACKNOWLEDGMENTS

I want to thank my exacting editor, Christine Dunbar, the Russian Library's board, and the production team at Columbia University Press for their confidence in my work, which I hope is not entirely misplaced. The advice of two anonymous peer reviewers proved invaluable. Robert Chandler, my first reader, offered insight and encouragement at every step, and Rose France, who understands Zoshchenko as well as anyone can, provided vital support near the end. I owe an immeasurable debt to Anna Glazer for, among other things, her peerless command of Soviet humor. And I save the last bow of thanks for the brilliant Jennifer Croft, who saved me from many embarrassments and, more importantly, laughed at just the right moments when reading the manuscript.

INTRODUCTION

Humor has an "evasiveness, which one had best respect," wrote E. B. White, a man who knew his way around a funny story.[1] Mikhail Zoshchenko, one of the greatest humorists of the Soviet era, exploited this essential evasiveness to the fullest. It's a quality that confused and even infuriated many Soviet critics of the 1920s and early 1930s, when Zoshchenko's popularity was at its height. In his review of Zoshchenko's 1927 collection *What the Nightingale Sang*—in which some of the "sentimental tales" in this volume were first collected—M. Ol'shevets accused the author of "restlessly tossing about," of failing to depict Soviet reality in its "true light."[2] Although this scathing review appeared in *Izvestiia*, one of the official organs of the Soviet regime, it didn't spell the end of Zoshchenko's career. Other critics believed his stories did more good than harm.[3]

It is lucky that the author's rise coincided with a period of relative liberalism in Soviet culture, a decade-long window of opportunity between the end of the Russian Civil War in 1921 and the emergence of a Stalinist monoculture, which culminated in 1934 with the enshrinement of Socialist Realism as the nation's artistic doctrine. This was also a period of radical social contradictions. The New Economic Policy (1921–1928), which Lenin introduced with the aim of stabilizing a war-ravaged economy, brought elements of capitalism—including, inadvertently, speculation and profiteering—into the workers' state.[4] This backward step was regarded as a shameful betrayal by many true believers in the communist cause, including the proletarian writers and artists who had hoped that the revolution would do away with the bourgeoisie and its culture once and for all.[5] Instead, members of the pre-Revolutionary bourgeoisie were now tolerated for their technical expertise, and NEP had created a whole new economic class, the so-called NEPmen, who made a living—and sometimes a killing—by privately manufacturing and selling goods.

Leaps forward and steps backward, impoverished bourgeois and nouveau riche NEPmen, utopian dreams and Soviet reality . . . Into this fraught sociocultural landscape stepped Zoshchenko, a satirist who hid behind so many masks that it was impossible to determine whom, exactly, he was mocking. Whose side was he on? Whose writer was he?

■ □ ■

That last question was posed by proletarian novelist Mikhail Chumandrin in 1930, in a speech reprinted in the journal *Zvezda*.[6] Although Chumandrin concluded that Zoshchenko was, ultimately, "with us," the very fact that the question needed to be raised spoke volumes. Zoshchenko really was, as Chumandrin claimed, "vague and difficult to pin down."[7] Indeed, in one of his many tongue-in-cheek autobiographical sketches, the author even refuses to pin down the place and time of his birth:

> I was born in 1895. In the previous century! That makes me terribly sad.
>
> I was born in the 19th century! Must be why I fail to treat our era with sufficient courtesy and romanticism—why I'm a humorist.
>
> I know precious little about myself.
>
> I don't even know where I was born. Either in Poltava or in St. Petersburg. One document says one thing, the other says another. One of them is obviously a fake. But it's hard to say which, since they're both pretty slapdash.
>
> There's some confusion over the year, too. One document claims it's 1895, the other claims it's 1896. A fake, no doubt about it.[8]

The truth is that the author was born in St. Petersburg—neither in 1895 nor in 1896, but on July 28, 1894—to a Ukrainian father and a Russian mother, both of whom were of noble origin.[9] The senior Zoshchenko, Mikhail Ivanovich, was an accomplished realist painter; his wife, Yelena Osipovna, née Surina, had been an actress before their marriage, and continued to dabble in literature. The couple had eight children. The junior Zoshchenko began to write at an early age, but he wouldn't make his debut until after the revolution of 1917.[10] In 1913 he entered the law faculty of St. Petersburg University, but was dismissed for nonpayment of fees in 1914. Soon war broke out in Europe, and after completing a course at the Pavlovsky Military Academy, Zoshchenko went off to the front. He served with valor, was injured and gassed, received four medals, and was promoted to the rank of captain. The gas attack, however, had seriously undermined his health, and he was sent to the reserves in 1917.

In the two years following the February revolution, Zoshchenko tried his hand at—by his own count—twelve professions, ranging from Commandant of the Main Telegraph and Post Office in Petrograd (as St. Petersburg was then called), to criminal investigator, apprentice cobbler, and instructor in rabbit and poultry breeding at a Soviet collective farm.[11] He attempted to enlist in the Red Army but was not accepted due to his ill health. It was at this point that he turned to literature, joining the writing workshops associated with the World Literature Publishing House (1918–1924), which had been established under the auspices of Maxim Gorky, partly in order to provide employment for struggling authors of all political affiliations. Zoshchenko quickly impressed his instructors and fellow students, including the literary critic Viktor Shklovsky. In 1921, he married and had a son, and also joined the Serapion Brotherhood, a literary group that drew together some of the most talented authors in Petrograd. The majority of the Serapions weren't members of the Bolshevik party, but they considered themselves to be "fellow travelers" with the regime.[12] In 1922, Zoshchenko staked out his own "fellow traveling" position in another autobiographical sketch:

> In general, being a writer's none too easy. Take ideology, for example . . . Nowadays a writer's got to have an ideology . . .
>
> . . .
>
> Well, that puts me in quite a pickle!
> What "precise ideology" could I possibly have, if there isn't a single party that attracts me as a whole?

. . .

I have no hatred for anyone—that's my "precise ideology."

You want more precision? Alright, here's more precision. In general thrust, I'm closest to the Bolsheviks. And I'm willing to bolshevize around with them.

. . .

But I'm not a communist (that is, not a Marxist), and I don't think I'll ever be one.[13]

Zoshchenko and the other Serapions could get away with this noncommittal stance in the 1920s. But even then they faced constant attacks from Marxist critics, especially those associated with the proletarian literary movement, who felt that Soviet culture should belong exclusively to the working class.

Ironically, the stories that made Zoshchenko extraordinarily popular parodied precisely the ham-handed manner and small-minded concerns of a would-be proletarian author. An uproarious gallimaufry of slang, dialect, misused cliché, and mangled bureaucratese, these little narratives—some of them no longer than a page—are the sharper-edged Soviet counterparts to Ring Lardner's spoofs of bush-league ballplayers and Damon Runyon's tales of Broadway hustlers and hoodlums.[14] They exposed Zoshchenko to more than his fair share of abuse from proletarian critics, but he was ever the moving target. Here is how he explained his artistic approach and affiliation in 1928:

I just want to make one confession. It may seem strange and unexpected. The fact is—I'm a proletarian writer. Rather, what I do in my stuff is parody an imaginary but genuine proletarian writer, who would exist under the present conditions and in the present social context. Of course, such a writer cannot exist, at least not at the moment. But when he does come to exist, then his community, his social context will improve greatly in every respect.

I'm only parodying. I'm temporarily filling in for the proletarian writer. That's why the themes of my stories are imbued with a naive philosophy, which won't fly over my readers' heads.[15]

This is a magical performance—or rather, a magic trick, like a game of three-card Monte. First Zoshchenko claims to be a proletarian writer, then he claims to parody that writer, and finally he reveals that the figure doesn't exist. One can't very well punish someone for making fun of a nonexistent subject, especially when he identifies with that subject. The poor critics were left empty-handed, while readers—proletarian and otherwise—ate the stories up.

Not content with burlesquing his imaginary proletarian scribbler, Zoshchenko also set his parodic sights on a slightly higher class of nonexistent litterateur: the "red Leo Tolstoy or Rabindranath Tagore," whose appearance was demanded by Soviet publishers.[16] The six "sentimental tales" in this volume are the result of Zoshchenko's effort to fashion such a figure from the crude material he saw all around him—the miserable remnants of the prerevolutionary petty intelligentsia.

■ □ ■

Our narrator, I. V. Kolenkorov, whose biography is sketched out in the second of four prefaces to the cycle, is doubly unsuited to the role of Soviet author.[17] In the first place, he is very much a man of the old regime—born in 1882, in a shabby provincial town, "to the petty bourgeois family of a ladies' tailor." Not only does he have little sense of what the revolution was all about, he's not even sure of when it took place; at the start of the first preface, we're told that these stories were written "at the very height of NEP and revolution"—but NEP, a reversion to capitalism, was hardly regarded as the "very height" of the revolution. And what is Kolenkorov's general take on the revolution's achievements? Often enough, despite his best efforts, he shows his cards: "Life in town changed tremendously. The revolution began to fashion a new way of life. But living wasn't easy. People had to fight for their right to live out their days."

As that poignantly tortured statement demonstrates, there's another obstacle on Kolenkorov's road to authorial glory: he's not so good at writing. In the third preface, we learn that Zoshchenko has gone to the trouble of correcting his protégé's "orthographic errors," but he has let stand "various sentimental undertones, whimpers, and a certain ideological vacillation in this or that direction"—to say nothing of Kolenkorov's assaults on good style. The budding author has never met an adjective or adverb he didn't want to intro-duce to another, for example, "Shocked and horrified at how quickly and rashly he had squandered his fortune, she would reproach him angrily and sharply for his foolish carelessness and eccentricity." Nor does our author have a particularly good grasp on figurative language. In the first tale, "Apollo and Tamara," Kolenkorov informs us that Fyodor Perepenchuk, "a medical attendant at the municipal recep-tion ward . . . was taken from us" some time ago, and then quickly corrects himself: "Of course, it isn't so much that he was taken from us as that he hanged himself."

This sort of gallows humor is Zoshchenko's specialty: he half-hides behind the comic mask of Kolenkorov—whom he outs, in the fourth preface, as "an imaginary person"—in order to deliver a devastating indictment of Soviet life, and of life in general.

■ □ ■

In the early 1930s, as the Soviet literary establishment grew increasingly monolithic, its tolerance for Zoshchenko's ironic games began to wear thin. Zoshchenko insisted that his projects of the 1930s were devoid of irony, but readers of his didactic *Youth Restored* (1933), in which he claimed to have discovered a cure for aging, and *Blue Book* (1935), an illustrative treatise on money, love, treachery, misfortune, and Soviet progress, can be forgiven for taking that assertion with a grain of salt. Yet he was clearly trying to satisfy, as best he could, the demands of the new cultural bosses. Perhaps the best evidence of this aspiration is his contribution to *The White Sea Canal* (1934), a propaganda volume dedicated to the eponymous Soviet construction project built by convicts in 1931–1933, as well as *Stories about Lenin* (1939), which were ostensibly meant to instill proper values in Soviet children.

Despite persistent criticism from certain quarters, Zoshchenko's efforts seem to have paid off. Unlike many of his colleagues, he was never arrested. His work continued to appear in print and was broadcast on the radio, and he was even awarded the Order of the Red Banner of Labor in 1939. But in 1943, during the Second World War, his luck began to turn. The serialized publication of his most ambitious project from that period, the autobiographical novella *Before Sunrise*, was halted due to hostile responses from critics and readers, who objected to its focus on personal psychology.[18] In 1946 he was viciously attacked by Andrey Zhdanov (1896–1948), whom Stalin had appointed to direct the Soviet Union's cultural policy, in a postwar crackdown that also targeted the poet Anna Akhmatova and the composers Dmitri Shostakovich and Sergei Prokofiev. Zoshchenko was expelled from the Soviet Writers' Union, and although he was admitted once more shortly after Stalin's death in 1953, his fall from grace did irreparable damage.[19] The depression from which he had suffered his whole life became crippling. Always a heavy smoker, he experienced strokelike symptoms from a nicotine overdose in the spring of 1958 and died of heart failure on July 22 of that year.

■ □ ■

For most of his life, Zoshchenko was an ill man, and his obsession with questions of health, both physical and mental, gave rise to some of his most intriguing work, like the self-analytic *Before Sunrise*. Illness and general human frailty also haunt the *Sentimental Tales*, hanging above them like a poisonous cloud. Paradoxically, the true measure of Zoshchenko's greatness as a humorist may be the fact that he still brings tears to our eyes. As E. B. White put it:

> Practically everyone is a manic depressive of sorts, with his up moments and his down moments, and you certainly don't have to be a humorist to taste the sadness of situation and mood. But there is often a rather fine line between laughing and crying, and if a humorous piece of writing brings a person to the point where his emotional responses are untrustworthy and seem likely to break over into the

opposite realm, it is because humor, like poetry, has an extra content. It plays close to the big hot fire which is Truth, and sometimes the reader feels the heat.[20]

I think of Zoshchenko's *Sentimental Tales* as shadow plays.[21] The characters are flimsy cutouts, manipulated by an inept puppeteer— but the play scripts are genuine tragedies. The shadows are cast by a big hot fire.

A NOTE ON THE TEXT

The six stories collected here were written between 1923 and 1929; five of them were first collected in a volume titled *What the Nightingale Sang: Sentimental Tales* (*O chem pel solovei. Sentimental'nye povesti*, 1927), along with two other stories—"Wisdom" ("Mudrost' ") and "The Goat" ("Koza"). The texts I've used for this translation appear in volume 3 of Zoshchenko's *Collected Works* (*Sobranie sochinenii* [Moscow: Vremia, 2008]), edited by I. .N. Sukhikh, and are drawn from Zoshchenko's *Selected Tales* (*Izbrannye povesti*) of 1936. The 1936 volume arranges the texts logically: The six stories narrated by I. V. Kolenkorov are grouped together and furnished with four prefaces, while "Wisdom" and "The Goat" appear in a separate cycle—*First Tales* (*Pervye povesti*)—along with "The Female Fish" ("Ryb'ia samka"). Unlike the six *Sentimental Tales* proper, "The Goat" has no framing narrator, while "Wisdom" appears to be narrated by some version of "Zoshchenko"; they are not the work of Kolenkorov. The four self-defensive—and contradictory—prefaces were radically revised from earlier texts and fashioned into a numbered series especially for the 1936 *Selected Tales*. I've chosen to limit the volume to the six

Kolenkorov tales and their four prefaces—that is, to Kolenkorov's collected works.

Zoshchenko made many revisions to his stories between editions—some minor, some more significant. Although I based the translation primarily on the 1936 text, I've also, in a few instances, restored passages that were likely cut for reasons of censorship. Earlier versions of the stories have been reprinted in *Stories and Feuilletons, 1922–1945. Sentimental Tales* (*Rasskazy i fel'etony, 1922–1945. Sentimental'nye povesti* [Moscow: OLMA-PRESS, 2004]).

SENTIMENTAL TALES

PREFACE TO THE FIRST EDITION

This book—this collection of sentimental tales—was written at the very height of NEP and revolution.

And so the reader is, of course, entitled to demand certain things of its author: real revolutionary content, grand subject matter, tasks of planetary significance, and heroic pathos—in a word, a full, lofty ideology.

The author would hate to see cash-strapped customers make unnecessary purchases, and so he hastens to announce, with a heavy heart, that this sentimental book contains only negligible amounts of heroism.

Its subject is, quite narrowly, the little man, the fellow in the street, in all his ugly glory.

But don't go condemning the author for choosing so petty a subject—for it appears he himself is a man of petty character. Can't be helped. People do the best they can with what they've been given.

One writer tosses onto his canvas, with the broadest of strokes, all sorts of episodes, another depicts the revolution, the third martial ritornellos, while the fourth occupies himself with amorous intrigues and challenges. Well, the present author, by virtue of the particular properties of his heart and of his humorous leanings, depicts mankind—how someone lives, what someone does, to what, let's say, this someone aspires.

The author acknowledges that, in our turbulent time, it is downright shameful, downright embarrassing to put forward such paltry ideas, such humdrum talk about a single insignificant person.

But that's no reason for critics to get all worked up and roil their precious blood. The author doesn't aim to slip his book into the list of our era's most ingenious works.

Perhaps that's why the author called his book sentimental.

Against the general backdrop of grand scales and ideas, these tales of weak little people, of everyday men and women—this book about miserable, fleeting life—will indeed, one must suppose, sound to certain critics like the shrill strains of some pitiful flute, nothing but offensively sentimental tripe.

Still, that can't be helped. One must record the situation as it stood in the early years of the revolution. Moreover, we have the temerity to think that these people—this above-mentioned stratum—still run rampant through the world. With that in mind, we bring to your esteemed attention this deficiently heroic book.

But if someone should claim that this opus lacks spirit—well, that just isn't the case. It has its fair share of spirit. It isn't excessively spirited, of course—but it has its fair share. The book's concluding pages simply bubble with absolute gaiety and heartfelt joy.

March 1927
I. V. Kolenkorov

PREFACE TO THE SECOND EDITION

In light of numerous inquiries we would like to inform the reader that the signature above—I. V. Kolenkorov—belongs to the genuine author of these sentimental tales.

Here is a brief biographical note regarding said author.

I. V. Kolenkorov is the brother of K. V. Kolenkorova, who is depicted so warmly and lovingly, along with other heroines, in the story "People." He was born in 1882 in the town of Torzhok (Tver Province), to the petit bourgeois family of a ladies' tailor. He received his education at home. In his younger years, he worked as a shepherd. In subsequent years, he performed in the theater. Then, at last, his lifelong dream came to fruition—he began to write poems and stories.

At present, I. V. Kolenkorov, who belongs to the right wing of the fellow travelers, is shifting allegiances. In the near future, he is likely to occupy a prominent place among writers of the natural school.

He composed these sentimental tales under the direction of the writer M. M. Zoshchenko, the head of a literary circle in which our venerable author moved for approximately five years.

At the present time, releasing this book, Ivan Vasilyevich extends his gratitude to Comrade Zoshchenko, wishing him good fortune in his burdensome pedagogical activity.

May 1928

K. Ch.[1]

PREFACE TO THE THIRD EDITION

In view of endless inquiries we would like to inform you that the writer M. Zoshchenko's role in this work has largely been confined to correcting orthographic errors and straightening ideological content. The greater part of the work belongs to the above-mentioned author, I. V. Kolenkorov. And so, in reality, the book's cover should have borne the name of Kolenkorov. However, I. V. Kolenkorov, not wishing to pass for a man of means, relinquished the honor to M. Zoshchenko. The fee, of course, went to Ivan Vasilyevich in full.

In the process of reporting this, we take the opportunity to declare that various sentimental undertones, whimpers, and a certain ideological vacillation in this or that direction ought not be attributed to the head of the literary circle, but, in part, to the author I. V. Kolenkorov, and, in part, to the personages depicted in these tales.

Here, in these pages, an entire gallery of now-departing characters will pass before your eyes.

The new, contemporary reader must know them, in order to see the departing way of life in all its manifestations.

July 1928
S. L.

PREFACE TO THE FOURTH EDITION

In view of past misunderstandings, the writer notifies his critic that the person who narrates these tales, is, so to speak, an imaginary person. He is a type—a middling intellectual who happens to live at the turn of two epochs.

Neurasthenia, ideological vacillation, major contradictions, and melancholy—that's what we had to bestow upon our "promoted worker," I. V. Kolenkorov.[1] Whereas the author—the writer M. M. Zoshchenko, son and brother to unhealthy men of this same sort— has, for his part, put all that behind him. At the present moment, he exhibits no contradictions. His soul is clear, bestrewn with blossoming roses. And if these roses wither from time to time, if tranquility departs from his heart—it is for wholly different reasons, of which the author will write at some later date.

In this case, we are dealing with a literary device.

The author implores the honorable critic to keep this tangle in mind before raising a hand against the defenseless writer.

April 1929
Mikh. Zoshchenko
Leningrad

APOLLO AND TAMARA

1

In a certain town, on Bolshaya Prolomnaya Street, there lived a free-lance artist—the pianist-for-hire Apollo Semyonovich, surname Perepenchuk.

Perepenchuk is a rare enough name in Russia, and readers might even assume that the hero of this tale is one Fyodor Perepenchuk, a medical attendant at the municipal reception ward, especially since both Perepenchuks lived at the same time and on the same street—and if their characters weren't exactly similar, we can at least say that, in terms of their somewhat skeptical attitude toward life and their general pattern of thought, the cuts of their jibs resonated.

But the medical attendant Fyodor Perepenchuk was taken from us at an earlier date. Of course, it isn't so much that he was taken from us as that he hanged himself. This happened just before the Fourth Congress.[1]

It was all over the papers at the time: Fyodor Perepenchuk, they said, a medical attendant at the municipal reception ward, committed suicide in the line of duty, owing to disillusionment with life . . .

There you have it, friends—that's the sort of hogwash our journos serve up these days. Disillusionment with life . . . Fyodor Perepenchuk and disillusionment with life . . . What a load of bunk. Pure hokum!

True, superficially speaking, we have here a man, a man who had, on occasion, pondered the senselessness of human existence and who died by his own hand. Sure, at first blush, that may look like disillusionment. But those who were close to Fyodor Perepenchuk, those who really knew him, would never talk such bunk.

Now, in the case of Apollo Perepenchuk, pianist-for-hire and musician—there you have disillusionment. There you have a man who lived in thoughtless enjoyment of his existence, but then, on account of purely material and physical causes, and as a result of various accidents and conflicts, lost his vigor and, in a manner of speaking, his taste for life. But let's not get ahead of ourselves. After all, our tale is about Apollo Perepenchuk.

Whereas Fyodor Perepenchuk . . . The whole force of his personality lay in the fact that he didn't arrive at his thoughts as a result of poverty, or of accidents and conflicts. No, his thoughts emerged from the mature, logical mental processes of a significant human being. He'd be a fitting subject for whole volumes of works, not just a single story. But not every writer would undertake that labor. Not every writer could serve as a biographer and, shall we say, a chronicler of the acts and thoughts of this extraordinary human being. The task would require a wordsmith possessed of the highest intelligence and greatest erudition, as well as knowledge of the minutest odds and ends of existence—the origin of man, the formation of the universe, all manner of philosophies, the theory of relativity and a bunch of other theories besides, where this and that star is located, and even the chronology of historical events. That's what you'd need to get a handle on the personality of Fyodor Perepenchuk.

And in this respect Apollo Perepenchuk is no match for Fyodor Perepenchuk.

Compared to Fyodor Perepenchuk, Apollo Perepenchuk was a trifling man—I'd even say a louse . . . No offense to his relatives. And anyway, he didn't leave behind any relatives in the Perepenchuk line, except for Adelaide Perepenchuk, his aunt on his father's side. And she—well, she doesn't exactly have a grasp of belles lettres. So let her take all the offense she wants.

Nor did he leave behind any friends. Yes, people like Fyodor and Apollo Perepenchuk aren't ones for friends. Fyodor never had any to begin with, and Apollo lost the friends he had when he fell into poverty.

How could Fyodor Perepenchuk have had friends? He disliked people—despised them, really—and led a closed-off, one could even say austere, life. And if ever he talked to people, it was in order to express, automatically, the views he had accumulated, not to hear cheers or criticism.

And who, no matter how highly intelligent, could have responded to his proud thoughts?

"Why does man exist? Is there a purpose to man's life—and if there isn't, then is life itself not, generally speaking, in part senseless?"

Of course, some assistant or full professor on the state's gravy train would reply, with unpleasant ease, that man exists in order to further culture and the happiness of the universe. But that's vague and unclear, and, for the common man, even disgusting. An answer like that gives rise to all sorts of surprising things: why, for example, do beetles or cuckoos exist? They do no good to anyone, least of all to the future of culture. And to what extent is man's life more important than that of a cuckoo—a bird that could live or not live, without changing the world one bit?

But here you'd need a pen of brilliance and a vast reserve of knowledge to reflect, at least partially, the grand conceptions of Fyodor Perepenchuk.

Perhaps we shouldn't even have disturbed the shade of this remarkable man. And we wouldn't have, had his thoughts not been, in later years, the final destination of his spiritual student and distant relative, Apollo Semyonovich Perepenchuk—pianist-for-hire, musician, and freelance artist who had once resided on Bolshaya Prolomnaya Street.

He had resided on that street a few years before the war and revolution.

2

The term pianist-for-hire isn't the least bit demeaning. Still, some people—including Apollo Semyonovich Perepenchuk himself—were reluctant to pronounce it in public, especially in mixed company, wrongly assuming that it might make the ladies blush. On those few occasions when Apollo Semyonovich did call himself a pianist-for-hire, he'd always add the word performer, or freelance artist, or some other qualification.

But this is not fair.

A pianist-for-hire is a musician, a pianist—even if, being in straitened material circumstances, he is forced to serve up his art as entertainment for the jolly crowd.

This profession isn't as valuable as, say, theater or painting, but it is, nevertheless, an art.

Of course, there are, in this profession, many little blind men, many deaf old women, who reduce the art to the level of an ordinary trade, senselessly hammering away with their fingers, banging out all kinds of polkas, polkettes, and majorettes.

But you couldn't very well place Apollo Semyonovich Perepenchuk in that category. His true calling, his artistic temperament, his lyricism, his inspiration—none of these fitted with prevailing notions of the pianist-for-hire's trade.

On top of that, Apollo Semyonovich Perepenchuk was sufficiently handsome and even refined. His face exuded inspiration and an unusual air of nobility. His lower lip, perennially bitten in pride, coupled with his haughty artistic profile, lent his figure the look of a sculpture.

Even his Adam's apple, his plain old Adam's apple—or, as it's sometimes called, the laryngeal prominence—which, when glimpsed on other men, is apt to trigger disgust or laughter, looked noble on Apollo Perepenchuk, whose head was invariably thrown proudly back. There was something Greek about that prominence.

And the flowing hair! The velvet blouse! The dark green tie hanging down to his waist! No way around it—the man was endowed with extraordinary beauty.

And those moments when he would arrive at a ball with his rapid gait and freeze like a statue in the doorway, as if surveying the whole of society with his haughty gaze . . . Yes, the man was irresistible. More than one woman shed copious tears over Apollo Perepenchuk. And how angrily other men shunned him! How they hid their wives from him—on the pretext that it was embarrassing, in their words, for the wife of a government official, say, to run around with some ivory-tickler.

And that unforgettable incident when the senior clerk at the Treasury Chamber received an anonymous letter explaining that his wife was on intimate terms with Apollo Perepenchuk! That hilarious scene—with said clerk lying in wait for Apollo Semyonovich for two hours, ready to pounce, only to be led astray by a flowing mane and mistakenly pummel the Secretary of the City Council . . .

Oh, there was indeed any amount of funny business! And the funniest thing was that all the scandals, the little notes, the ladies' tears were completely groundless. Graced with the countenance of a lothario, romancer, and destroyer of families, Apollo Semyonovich Perepenchuk was, on the contrary, an extremely timid and quiet man.

In fact, he avoided women, kept his distance from them, convinced that a true artist mustn't tie himself down to anything . . .

Yes, women wrote him notes and letters, attempting to arrange secret assignations and addressing him with terms of endearment and diminutives, but he was not to be moved.

He kept the notes and letters in a little box, taking them out in his spare time to examine them, number them, and bind them in little packs. But he lived in solitude, and was even, one could say, closed off. He loved to pronounce, at the least provocation: "Art comes first."

And when it came to art, Apollo Perepenchuk was far from last. There are, of course, virtuosos who can perform all kinds of different motifs using only the black keys. Apollo Perepenchuk couldn't hold a candle to those fellows. Still, he did have a waltz to his name—"The Dreams that Engulf Me" . . .

He used to perform this waltz quite successfully before huge audiences within the walls of the Merchants' Assembly Hall.

That was in the year under discussion—the year of his greatest glory and fame. Another of his works, the unfinished "Fantaisie réale"—composed in major tones, but not deprived thereby of charming lyricism—belongs to the same period. This "Fantaisie réale" was dedicated to a certain Tamara Omelchenko, the maiden who would play so crucial and fatal a role in the life of Apollo Semyonovich Perepenchuk.

3

But here the author must show his hand to his dear readers. The author assures them that he will in no way distort the events of which he writes. On the contrary, he will reconstruct them exactly as they occurred, with utmost fidelity to the tiniest details, such as the physical appearance of the protagonists, their ways of thinking, and even sentimental motifs, which the author would rather ignore.

The author pledges to his dear readers that when he recalls certain sentimental scenes—say, the heroine crying over a portrait, or the same heroine mending Apollo Perepenchuk's torn tunic, or, finally, Aunt Adelaide Perepenchuk announcing the sale of Apollo Semyonovich's wardrobe—he does so with extraordinary sorrow and a painful sense of anxiety.

These descriptions are, so to speak, contrary to the author's taste, but he offers them for the sake of truth. For the sake of truth, the author even uses his protagonists' actual names. The reader mustn't think that the author has graced his protagonists with such rare,

exceptional names—Tamara and Apollo—out of aesthetic considerations. No, these people were actually called Tamara and Apollo.
And that's really no surprise. The author happens to know for certain
that all the girls of seventeen or eighteen on Bolshaya Prolomnaya
Street were without exception Tamaras or Irinas.

And there's a perfectly good explanation for this coincidence.
Seventeen years earlier, a regiment of hussars was stationed in town.
And this regiment was so glorious, the hussars so strapping—
affecting the citizenry so profoundly from the aesthetic point of
view—that all the female babies born at the time were named
Tamara or Irina, following the example set by the governor's wife.

And so, in that happy year of dizzying successes, Apollo Semyonovich Perepenchuk first met and fell in love with the maiden
Tamara Omelchenko.

She wasn't quite eighteen then. And you couldn't exactly call her
a beauty, but she was better than a beauty—there was such noble
roundness to all her shapes, such a floating quality to her gait, and
such a charming air of tender youth about her. Any man who walked
past her, be it on the street or even at a public gathering, inevitably
called her a donut, sweet bun, or cream puff, gazing at her with acute
attention and pleasure.

That same year she also fell in love with Apollo Semyonovich
Perepenchuk.

They met at a ball within the walls of the Merchants' Assembly
Hall. This happened at the start of the European worldwide war.
She was struck by his unusually noble appearance, the lower lip bitten
in pride. He was enraptured by her pristine freshness.

That evening he was in particularly fine form. He pounded on the
piano with all the force of his inspiration, so that the foreman finally

had to come over and ask him to play a bit more quietly, making out that he was upsetting the club's full members.

At this moment Apollo Perepenchuk realized just how insignificant and miserable a person he really was. Attached, by virtue of his profession, to a musical instrument, he couldn't even walk over to the maiden he admired. With these thoughts weighing on his mind, he expressed through sounds all the anguish and despair of a man in bondage.

Tamara, meanwhile, was whirled about in waltzes and mazurkas by many respectable gentlemen, but her eyes always came to rest on the inspired mien of Apollo Perepenchuk.

And at the end of the evening, overcoming her girlish timidity, she herself walked over to the piano and asked him to play one of his favorite tunes. He played the waltz "The Dreams That Engulf Me."

That waltz sealed the deal. Seized with the trembling of first love, she took his hand and pressed it to her lips.

Vicious gossip about Apollo Perepenchuk's latest "union" spread like wildfire through the entire premises of the Merchants' club. No one bothered to conceal their curiosity. People sauntered past the couple, smirking and giggling. Even those who were already pulling on their coats shed their furs and went back upstairs to verify the juicy rumors with their own eyes.

Thus began the love affair.

Apollo Perepenchuk and Tamara took to meeting on holidays at the corner of Prolomnaya and Kirpichny. They would promenade into the evening hours, talking of their love and of that extraordinary, unforgettable evening when they had first met, recalling its every detail, embellishing everything, and admiring each other.

This went on until autumn.

But when Apollo Semyonovich Perepenchuk, wearing his finest jacket and carrying a bouquet of oleander and a box of Lenten sugar,[2] came to ask for Tamara's hand, she refused him with the prudence of a mature woman who knows her worth, despite the appeals of her mother and of the Omelchenko ménage.

"Mother dearest," she said, "yes, I love Apollo with all the passion of a maiden's heart, but I shall not marry him now. When he becomes a famous musician, when glory kneels at his feet, I'll go to him myself. And I believe that day will come soon. I believe he will be well known, famous, able to provide well for his wife."

Apollo Perepenchuk was present during these remarks, at first bowing his head.

All evening he wept at her feet, kissing her knees with unspeakable passion and longing. But she was insistent. She was loath to take risks, fearing poverty and insecurity. She didn't want to drag out her life in misery, as almost all people do.

Then Apollo Perepenchuk dashed off for home. For a few days he dwelled in some kind of fog, some kind of frenzy, trying to devise some way of becoming a famous, renowned musician. But what had once seemed plain and simple now appeared to be extraordinarily difficult, if not impossible.

Various plans flashed through his mind: to go to another city, give up music, quit the arts, and seek his fortune and glory in another profession, in another field, becoming, say, a courageous aviator, looping the loop over his hometown, above his beloved's roof, or perhaps becoming an inventor, an explorer, a surgeon . . . But these were all merely dreams. Apollo Perepenchuk would puncture each and every one of them, deriding his own imagination.

He sent his composition, the waltz "The Dreams That Engulf Me," to Petersburg, but the manuscript's fate remains unknown. Perhaps it got lost in the mail, or maybe someone appropriated it, passing it off as their own composition—we simply don't know. It was never published or performed.

Today even its motif is all but lost to history. Only Aunt Adelaide Perepenchuk keeps it in her memory. Oh, how she loved to sing that waltz!

Another of Apollo Perepenchuk's compositions belongs to this period—the unfinished "Fantaisie réale." It remains unfinished not because of creative ineptitude, but because our poor hero was struck by another blow.

Apollo Semyonovich was drafted into the army as a noncombat soldier.

What he had dreamt of was now a reality: he could leave and seek his fortune elsewhere.

In December of 1916 Apollo Perepenchuk came to say good-bye to his beloved.

Even the most cynical townsfolk, the stoniest hearts wept as they gazed at the couple's tender parting.

Bidding farewell, Apollo Perepenchuk declared solemnly that he would return either as a renowned, famous man or not at all. He proclaimed that neither war nor anything else would stand in the way of his ambition.

And the maiden, laughing gratefully through her tears, said that she had complete faith in him. She affirmed that she would become his wife when he returned as a man who could ensure their mutual happiness.

4

And so a few years—a little over four, to be exact—passed since Apollo Semyonovich Perepenchuk entered the army.

This was a time of enormous changes. Social ideas significantly altered and overturned our former way of life. Many fine people departed the earth to join their ancestors in eternity. Kuzma Lvovich Goryushkin, for example, a former trustee of the school district and a most good-natured, cultured man, was done in by typhus. Semyon Semyonovich Petukhov, another superb fellow who didn't mind a drink or two, also died. And the death of medical attendant Fyodor Perepenchuk occurred during this same period.

Life in town changed tremendously. The revolution began to fashion a new way of life. But living wasn't easy. People had to fight for their right to live out their days.

And no one during this time gave a single thought to Apollo Semyonovich Perepenchuk. Well, maybe Tamara Omelchenko did, once or twice, and maybe his aunt Adelaide Perepenchuk. Of course, perhaps some other maiden thought of him as well—but simply as a romantic hero, not as a pianist-for-hire and musician. No one recalled him as a pianist-for-hire, and no one regretted his absence. There were no more pianists-for-hire in town, nor was there any need of them. Under the new conditions, many professions became obsolete, and pianist-for-hire was one such dying trade.

Maestro Solomon Belenky now provided the entertainment at all gatherings, with his two first violins, cello, and double bass. At all parties, charity balls, weddings, and christenings this man, who had appeared out of nowhere, worked with a success that, we have to admit, was simply dizzying. Everyone loved him. And it's true:

no one could twirl a violin in his hands like Maestro Belenky, turning it around during a rest and hitting its sounding board with his bow. Moreover, he played a medley of favorite motifs and could perform various dances of both domestic and transatlantic origin, such as the "tremutar" and the "bear." On top of that, the smile that never abandoned his face, in combination with a certain good-natured winking at the dancers, finally conspired to make him a favorite of the jolly public. He was, so to speak, an artist of our time. And he drove Apollo Semenovich Perepenchuk out of the townsfolk's minds, trampling him into the dust.

And that very year, when Tamara began to forget Apollo Perepenchuk, and when Aunt Adelaide Perepenchuk, thinking her nephew killed in action, hung a notice on her gate announcing to all and sundry the sale of Apollo Perepenchuk's wardrobe, including: two pairs of lightly worn trousers, a velvet jacket with a dark green tie, a piqué vest, and a few other items—that same year Apollo Perepenchuk returned to his hometown.

He rode in a freight car with other soldiers and lay on his bunk the whole way, his head resting on his bag. He looked sick. He had changed terribly. The soldier's overcoat, torn and burnt on the back, the army boots, the baggy khaki trousers, the hoarse voice—all these rendered him completely unrecognizable. He was a different man.

Constant contact with a clarinet had even stretched his lip, formerly bitten in pride, into a thin ribbon.

No one ever did learn what disaster had befallen him. Had there even been a disaster? In all likelihood, there hadn't been any disaster—just life, plain, simple life, from which only two people out of a thousand ever manage to get back on their feet, while others just wait it out.

He never told anyone about his experiences over those five years, of what he had done in the hope of returning in glory and honor.

Only the clarinet he brought back with him gave people reason to suspect that he had, as before, sought glory in the realm of art. He must have been a musician in some regimental band. But nothing is known for certain. He wrote no letters home, apparently not wanting to report on the minor facts of his life.

In other words, a mystery.

We only know that he returned not only without fame but also sick and hungry—a changed man, with wrinkles on his forehead, an elongated nose, faded eyes, and his head bowed low.

He returned to his aunt's house like a thief. Like a thief, he ran through the streets from the station, lest he be seen. But if anyone had seen him, they wouldn't have recognized him. There was nothing of the old Apollo Perepenchuk in him. He was a whole other Apollo Perepenchuk.

His return itself was a frightful scene. He had barely crossed the threshold when a new blow came down upon his head. His possessions, his lovely possessions—the velvet jacket, the trousers, the vest—had all perished irrevocably. Aunt Adelaide Perepenchuk had sold everything, down to his safety razor.

Apollo Semyonovich heard out his aunt's sobs somewhat indifferently, with a measure of disgust. He offered no reproof, only asking once more about the velvet jacket, and then dashed out to see Tamara.

He raced to her along Bolshaya Prolomnaya, panting, without a thought in his head. All the dogs ran out to meet him, barking and snapping at his ragged trousers.

Finally, after one last exertion—her home, Tamara's home . . . Apollo Perepenchuk banged his fist on the door.

Tamara took fright at the sight of him, trying to understand—at once, this very minute—what had befallen him. Seeing his tattered tunic and haggard face—she understood.

He gazed intently, piercingly into her eyes, trying to penetrate her thoughts, to understand. But he did not understand.

They stood facing each other for a long time, not saying a word. Then he got down on his knees, and, not knowing what to say, wept quietly. She also began to weep, sobbing and sniffling like a child.

After a while, she sat down in a chair, and Apollo, crouching at her feet, babbled all kinds of nonsense. Tamara stared at him but understood nothing and saw nothing. All she saw was his soiled face, his matted hair, and his torn tunic. Her tender little heart, the heart of a sensible woman, was wrung to the utmost. She brought out her sewing kit and asked him, through her tears, to thread a needle. Then she began to mend his tunic, occasionally shaking her head in reproach.

But here the author must interject and say that he's no snot-nosed kid, to go on this way, describing sentimental scenes. And although there isn't much of that stuff left, the author must move on to the hero's psychology, deliberately omitting two or three intimate, sentimental details, such as: Tamara combing Apollo's matted hair, wiping his haggard face with a towel, and sprinkling him with *Persian Lilac* . . .[3] The author states unequivocally that he has no truck with these details and is interested solely in psychology.

And so, thanks to this show of affection on Tamara's part, Apollo Perepenchuk came to believe that all was as before, that she still loved him. He rushed to her with a cry of delight, attempting to lock her in his embrace.

But, with a frown, she declared:

"Kind Apollo Semyonovich, I believe I said far too much to you in those days . . . I hope you didn't take my innocent girlish prattling at face value."

He remained on his knees, straining to understand her words. She got up, crossed the room, and said testily:

"Perhaps I have wronged you, but I will not be your wife."

Apollo Perepenchuk went back to his aunt's house, where he realized that his old life was gone forever—and that it had all been ridiculous and naïve from the start. His desire to become a great musician, a well-known, famous man, had been ridiculous and naïve. And he realized that he had lived his entire life in the wrong way—doing the wrong things, saying the wrong things . . . But he still hadn't the faintest idea of what the right things might have been.

As he lay down to sleep, he grinned bitterly—just as medical assistant Fyodor Perepenchuk had grinned bitterly in his time, attempting, at long last, to understand, to penetrate the essence of natural phenomena.

5

Before long Apollo Semyonovich Perepenchuk sank deep into poverty. Moreover, this was the poverty, even the penury, of a man who had lost all hope of bettering his situation. Of course, he had been totally broke ever since his return, but at first he had refused to confess his abject poverty.

Now he would say to Aunt Adelaide Perepenchuk with an evil grin: "Auntie, I'm as poor as a Spanish beggar."

His aunt, feeling great guilt before him, would try to comfort him, calm him, encourage him, saying that all was not lost, that his whole life still lay ahead, that she would replace the dark green tie she had sold with a charming purple one, fashioned from the bodice of her evening dress, and that Ripkin, a ladies' tailor of her acquaintance, would gladly take up the task of sewing him a velvet jacket on the cheap.

But Apollo Perepenchuk only grinned in response.

He didn't take a single step, made no attempt whatsoever to change, to restore his earlier way of life about town. To be fair, he only gave up in earnest after he learned that Maestro Solomon Belenky now presided over every urban gathering. Prior to that, all kinds of vague dreams and elusive plans had jostled in his excited mind.

Maestro Solomon Belenky and the disappearance of the velvet jacket conspired to transform Apollo Perepenchuk into a mere will-less contemplator.

He lay in bed all day, going out into the street only to look for a cigarette butt or to ask a passerby for a pinch of tobacco. Aunt Adelaide kept him fed.

Sometimes he would get out of bed, pull his clarinet from its cloth case, and play a bit. But in his music there was no trace of melody, nor even of individual notes—it was like the terrifying demonic howl of an animal.

And every time he would play, a change would come to Aunt Adelaide Perepenchuk's face. She would retrieve various canisters and jars of drugs and smelling salts from her cupboard, then lie down with a muffled moan.

Apollo Semyonovich would eventually toss aside his clarinet and again seek solace in bed.

He lay in shrewd contemplation, subject to the same thoughts that had formerly troubled Fyodor Perepenchuk. And his other thoughts, in terms of force and depth, were in no way inferior to those of his considerable namesake. He contemplated human existence, the fact that man is as ridiculous and unnecessary as a beetle or a cuckoo, and that all people, the whole world over, must change their lives in order to find peace and happiness, in order to avoid the suffering that had befallen him. At one point it seemed to him he had discovered, at long last, how man ought to live. Some thought touched his mind and disappeared again without quite taking shape.

This started insignificantly enough. Apollo Perepenchuk asked Aunt Adelaide:

"What do you think, Auntie, does man have a soul?"

"Yes," the aunt said. "Certainly."

"But what about monkeys? Monkeys are humanlike . . . No worse than humans. Do you suppose monkeys have souls, Auntie?"

"I suppose that monkeys have souls," the aunt said, "since they're humanlike."

Apollo Perepenchuk suddenly grew agitated. He was stricken by a bold thought.

"Excuse me, Auntie," he said. "If monkeys have souls, then dogs surely have them. Dogs are no worse than monkeys. And if dogs have souls, then so do cats—and rats, and flies, and even worms . . ."

"That's enough!" the aunt demanded. "You're blaspheming."

"Not at all, Auntie," Apollo Perepenchuk replied. "Not in the least. I'm just stating the facts . . . So, by your logic, worms have souls . . .

Say I take a worm, then, Auntie, and cut it in half, right down the middle . . . Now imagine, Auntie, that each half goes on living on its own. So? According to you, Auntie, that's a soul split in two! What kind of soul is that?"

"Leave me be," the aunt implored and gazed at Apollo Semyonovich with frightened eyes.

"No, let me finish!" cried Perepenchuk. "So there's no soul. Man has no soul. Man is bone and meat . . . He dies like the lowest beast, and is born like a beast. Only he lives on fantasies. But he must live differently . . ."

Except that Apollo Semyonovich couldn't explain to his aunt how man ought to live—because he simply didn't know. Yet he had been shaken by his thoughts. It seemed he had begun to understand something. But then his mind grew confused, jumbled. He had to admit that, in fact, he had no idea how a man ought to live in order to avoid feeling what he himself now felt. What did he feel, exactly? He felt his game was up, that life was calmly marching on without him.

For several days he paced the room in a state of extreme agitation. And on the day this agitation reached its highest point of tension, Aunt Adelaide brought in a letter addressed to Apollo Semyonovich Perepenchuk. The letter was from Tamara.

With the affectations of a flirtatious woman, she wrote in a sad lyric tone that she was preparing to marry a certain foreign merchant named Glob, and that, in taking this step, she did not wish Apollo Perepenchuk to think badly of her. She issued a most humble apology for all the things she had done to him; she was asking forgiveness, knowing what a mortal blow she had struck him.

Apollo Perepenchuk laughed quietly as he read the letter. Yet her unshakable conviction that he, Apollo Perepenchuk, was perishing on her account truly stunned him. Contemplating this, he suddenly realized that he needed nothing, not even her, on whose account he was perishing. And he also realized, clearly and finally, that he was perishing not on her account, but because he hadn't lived as he ought to have lived. But then his mind grew confused and jumbled again.

And he wanted to go to her immediately, to say that it was not she who was to blame—that he alone was to blame, that he had made some mistake in his life.

But he didn't go, because he didn't know what that mistake had been.

6

A week later Apollo Semyonovich Perepenchuk paid Tamara a visit. It all happened unexpectedly. One night he quietly put on his clothes, told Aunt Adelaide that he had a headache and wanted to take a walk, then left the house. He walked for a long time, wandering aimlessly through the streets, with no intention of going to see Tamara. Extraordinary musings on the meaninglessness of existence gave him no peace. He took off his cap and wandered the streets, occasionally halting beside dark wooden houses and peering into their lighted windows, attempting to understand, to penetrate, to see how people lived—to get at the nature of their existence. Through the lighted windows he saw men in suspenders sitting at tables, women standing near samovars, children . . . Some men were playing cards; others sat without moving, staring blankly at flames. Some women washed dishes, or sewed—and that was about it. Many ate, opening their mouths wide without making a sound. And despite the double panes, it seemed to Apollo Perepenchuk that he could hear them champ and chew.

Apollo Semyonovich went from house to house and before he knew it, there he was, at Tamara's residence.

He pressed against the window to her room. Tamara lay on the couch—apparently asleep. Suddenly, to his own surprise, Apollo Semyonovich rapped on the glass with his fingers.

Tamara shivered, leapt up, and listened intently. Then she went to the window, trying to make out in the darkness who it was that had knocked. But she could not, and so she shouted: "Who is it?"

Apollo Semyonovich was silent.

She ran out into the street, recognized him, and brought him into the house. She began to lecture him angrily, telling him that he had no business coming here, that it was all over between them—and hadn't her written apologies been enough?...

Apollo Perepenchuk gazed at her beautiful face, thinking that there was no point in telling her that she wasn't to blame, that he alone was to blame, that he had conducted his life in the wrong way. She wouldn't understand, and wouldn't want to understand, because this situation seemed to give her some sort of pleasure, and perhaps even boosted her pride.

He wanted to go, but something stopped him. For a long time he stood in the middle of the room, thinking intensely. Then a strange calm came over him. He cast his eyes around Tamara's room, smiled blankly, and left.

He went out into the street, walked two blocks, put on his cap— and stopped.

"That thought—what had it been?"

At that moment, when he had stood in her room, some happy thought had flashed across his mind. But he had forgotten it . . . Some thought, some conclusion that had, for a moment, brought him calm and clarity.

Apollo Perepenchuk tried to recollect every detail, every word. Was it that he should leave? No . . . Become a clerk? No . . . He had forgotten.

So he raced back to her house. Yes, of course, he must get back inside her home, her room, now, this very minute—there, standing in that same spot, he'd recall that blasted thought.

He went up to her door, intending to knock. But he noticed that the door was open. No one had locked it behind him. He quietly walked down the hall, unnoticed, and stopped on the threshold of Tamara's room.

Tamara was weeping, her face buried in her pillow. In her hand she held a photograph—a portrait of him, Apollo Perepenchuk.

Let the reader cry all he wants—the author couldn't care less. He remains unmoved, proceeding impassively to further developments.

Apollo Perepenchuk looked at Tamara, at the photograph in her hand, at the window. He looked at the flower on the table, at the little vase with some dried herbs and grasses, and suddenly it came to him.

"Yes!"

Tamara screamed when she saw him. He raced off, his boots stamping down the hall. Someone from the kitchen rushed after him.

Apollo Semyonovich ran out of the house. He walked quickly down Prolomnaya Street. Then he began running again. He fell in the soft snow. Tripped. Got up. Ran on further.

"I've found that thought!"

He ran a long time, gasping for breath. The cap fell from his head, but he raced on without stopping to find it. The city was quiet. It was the dead of night. Perepenchuk kept running.

At last he reached the outskirts of town. The suburbs. Fences. Railroad signal. Huts. Side ditch. Railway bed.

Apollo Perepenchuk collapsed. He crawled a bit farther, reached the rails, then lay still.

"My thought. I've found it."

He lay in the soft snow. His heart kept skipping beats. He felt he was dying.

A man holding a lantern walked past him twice, then came back and nudged him in the ribs with his foot.

"What's with you?" said the man with the lantern. "Whatcha lyin' there for?"

Perepenchuk didn't respond.

"Whatcha lyin' there for?" the man repeated in a frightened tone. The lantern shook in his hand.

Apollo Semyonovich raised his head and sat up.

"People are good . . . People are good," he said.

"What people?" the man said quietly. "Whatcha ramblin' about? Come on, now, let's go to my hut. I'm the switchman . . ."

The man took him by the hand and led him to his hut.

"People are good . . . People are good," Perepenchuk kept muttering.

They went into the hut. It was stuffy. A table. A lamp. A samovar. Sitting at the table, a peasant in an unbuttoned coat. A woman crumbling sugar with a pair of tongs.

Perepenchuk sat down on a bench. His teeth were chattering.

"So why'd you go and lie down out there, eh?" the switchman asked again, winking at the man in the coat. "Lookin' for death, were ya? Or did ya wanna go and tear up them rails?"

"What did he do?" asked the man in the coat. "Lie down on the rails?"

"That's what he did," said the switchman. "I'm out there with my lantern, and there he is, the asshole, lyin' there like a baby, his mug stuck right up against the rail."

"Hm," said the man in the coat. "Bastard."

"You back off," said the woman. "Don't you go yellin' at him. You see the fella's shakin'. He ain't shakin' from joy. Have some tea, fella . . ."

Apollo Perepenchuk drank, his teeth knocking against the glass.

"People are good . . ."

"Hold on," said the switchman, winking at the man in the coat again and, for some reason, elbowing him in the side. "I'm gonna ask 'im some questions, orderly and official-like."

Apollo Semyonovich sat motionless.

"Answer in order, like on paper," the switchman said sternly. "Family name."

"Perepenchuk," said Apollo Semyonovich.

"Never heard of it. Age?"

"Thirty-two."

"Prime of life," the man said with inexplicable satisfaction. "Me, I'm in my fifty-first year . . . Now that's an age . . . Out of work?"

"Out of work . . ."

The switchman grinned and winked again.

"Not good," he said. "Well, you got any skill? Know any skill?"

"No . . ."

"Not good," the switchman said, shaking his head. "How you gonna live without handi-skills, fella? I tell ya, that ain't no good at all. A man's gotta know a handi-skill. Take me—I'm a watchman, a switchman. But say they run me out—cutbacks or some such . . . Well, that won't be the end of me. I know how to work boots. I'll work boots till my arms fall off, and I won't come to grief. Hell, I'll twist ropes with my teeth. Yes, that's me. But you ain't got no handi-skill. Can't do a doggone thing . . . How you gonna live?"

"An aristocrat, this one," the man in the coat scoffed. "Blood's too blue . . . Can't live. They just go and stick their snouts in rails."

Apollo Perepenchuk got to his feet. He wanted to leave. But the switchman wouldn't let him:

"Sit down. I'll set you up with a splendid job."

He winked at the man in the coat and said:

"Vasya, why dontcha take the fella on? You do nice, quiet work—anyone can understand. Why let the poor fella croak?"

"All right," the man said, buttoning his coat. "Listen here, citizen: you come to the Annunciation Cemetery and ask the fella in charge if I'm around."

"Take 'im with ya now, Vasya," the woman said. "You never know."

"All right," the man said, getting up and putting on his hat. "Well, let's go, then. So long, now."

The man left the hut with Apollo Perepenchuk.

7

Apollo Semyonovich Perepenchuk entered the third and last period of his life—he assumed the position of a freelance gravedigger.

For almost a full year Apollo Semyonovich labored at the Annunciation Cemetery. Once again, he underwent a remarkable change.

He went about in yellow leg wrappings, a half-coat, and a brass badge on his chest—No. 3. His calm, thoughtless face exuded quiet bliss. All wrinkles, blemishes, and freckles vanished from his countenance. His nose took on its former shape. It was only that his eyes would occasionally fix without blinking on some object—on a single point on that object—no longer seeing or noticing anything else.

At those moments Apollo would contemplate, or rather, recall his life, the path he had traveled, and then his calm face would grow dark. But these recollections would come over him against his will—he was trying to rid his mind of all thought. He acknowledged that he had no sense of what he ought to have done, of what mistake he had made in his life. And had there really been a mistake? Perhaps there hadn't. Perhaps it was all just life—simple, stark, and plain—which allows only two or three people out of a thousand to smile and enjoy themselves.

However, all these sorrows were now behind him. A spirit of happy tranquility never again left Apollo Semyonovich. Every morning, at the usual hour, he would come to work with a shovel in his hand, and while digging the earth and straightening the sides of the graves, he'd well up with enthusiasm at the silence and charm of his new life.

On summer days, after working two hours or more without a break, he would lie down on the grass or on the warm, freshly dug earth, and would gaze without moving at the fleecy clouds, or follow the flight of some little birdie, or simply hearken to the rustle of the Annunciation's pines. Recalling his past, Apollo Perepenchuk reflected that he had never felt such peace in all his life, that he had never lain in the grass and had never known that freshly dug earth was warm and smelled sweeter than French powder or any drawing room. And then he would smile a calm, full smile, happy at being alive and wanting to live on.

But one day Apollo Semyonovich Perepenchuk spotted Tamara walking arm in arm with some fairly important-looking foreigner. They were strolling down the path of Saint Blessed Xenia, blithely prattling about this or that.

Apollo Perepenchuk snuck after them, crouching behind graves and crosses like an animal. The couple strolled through the cemetery for a long time, then found a dilapidated bench and sat down, squeezing each other's hands.

Apollo Perepenchuk fled from the scene.

But that was an isolated incident. Life went on as before, calm and quiet. The days followed one another, and nothing disturbed their calm. Apollo Semyonovich worked, ate, lay in the grass, and slept . . . Occasionally he would stroll through the cemetery, read the touching or clumsy inscriptions on the headstones, sit down on this or that forgotten grave, and stay there for a while, thinking of nothing.

On the nineteenth of September, according to the new calendar, Apollo Semyonovich Perepenchuk succumbed to a heart rupture while working on one of the graves.

As it happens, Tamara Glob, née Omelchenko, had died in childbirth on the seventeenth of September—that is, two days before his own death.

Alas, Apollo Semyonovich Perepenchuk never heard about this.

March 1923

PEOPLE

1

Strange things are afoot in literature these days! If an author should write a tale about contemporary events—why, that author is lavished with praise from all sides. The critics applaud him, the readers sympathize.

Now say that same author manages to pin some public theme, some precious little social idea onto this tale of his—well, said author lands himself on the receiving end of fame, popularity, all kinds of respect. He gets his picture in all the weekly papers. And the publishers pay him in gold—no less than a hundred rubles a sheet.

Well, in our worthless opinion, this hundred rubles a sheet is clearly and totally unjust.

After all, in order to write a tale about contemporary events, one needs access to the appropriate geography—that is, the author must be located in the major centers or capitals of the republic, where the vast majority of historical events happen to take place.

But not every author has that geography at his disposal—not every author has the material opportunity to reside with his family in the major cities and capitals.

Therein lies the stumbling block and the cause of injustice.

One author resides in Moscow, and, so to speak, witnesses with his own eyes the whole round of events involving his heroes and great leaders, while another, by virtue of family circumstances, drags out a miserable existence in some provincial town where nothing particularly heroic has ever happened or ever will.

So how is our author supposed to get his hands on major world events, contemporary ideas, and significant heroes?

Would you have him tell lies? Or would you have him rely on the absurd, inaccurate rumors his comrades bring back from the capital?

No, no, and no! The author loves and respects belles lettres too much to base his compositions on old wives' tales and unverified rumors.

Of course, some enlightened critic who can prattle in six foreign tongues may urge the author not to shun the minor heroes and little provincial scenes taking place all around him. Such a critic may even insist that it's preferable to sketch out little colorful etudes peopled with insignificant provincial types.

Dear critic, keep your silly comments to yourself! The author has thought it all through long before you came along. Yes, he's traveled down every road and worn out more than a few pairs of boots. He'll have you know that he's inscribed every name more or less worthy of attention on a separate piece of paper, adding various comments and a nota bene or two. But he keeps coming up empty! Forget remarkable heroes—there isn't even a single mediocrity whose story would be the least bit interesting or instructive. Nothing but small fry, piffle, zeroes who have no place in belles lettres, no place in the contemporary heroic scheme of things.

Of course, the author would still rather confine himself to an altogether small scale, to an altogether insignificant hero with all his trifling passions and experiences, rather than letting loose and spinning tall tales about some altogether nonexistent person. The author has neither the insolence nor the imagination for that task.

In addition, the author considers himself a member of the only honest literary school—the naturalists—who will determine the future course of Russian belles lettres. But even if the author didn't consider himself a member of this school, he would still find it, shall we say, difficult to write about an unfamiliar person. He might overshoot the mark and bungle up his psychological analysis—or he might skip over some little detail, so that the reader hits a dead end and is forced to wonder at the carelessness of contemporary writers.

Hence, by virtue of the reasons outlined above, and also due to certain restrictive material circumstances, the author begins his contemporary tale, but he does so with a warning: the tale's hero is trifling and unimportant, perhaps unworthy of the attention of today's pampered public. As the reader might have guessed, this hero is Ivan Ivanovich Belokopytov.

The author would never have considered expending his gift for empathy on such a figure, but the demand for contemporary tales has forced his hand. Grudgingly, he takes up the pen and begins the tale of Belokopytov.

This will be a somewhat melancholy tale of the collapse of every possible philosophical system, of man's destruction, of the essential meaninglessness of human culture, and of how easily that culture can vanish. It will narrate the collapse of idealistic philosophy.

On this plane, Ivan Ivanovich Belokopytov may indeed have been a rather curious and significant specimen. The author advises the reader not to attach much importance to any other plane, and certainly not to empathize with the hero's base, beastly emotions and animal instincts.

And so the author takes up the pen and begins his contemporary tale.

The tale is not so very rich in personae: Ivan Ivanovich Belokopytov—lean, thirty-seven years of age, non-Party; his wife, Nina Osipovna Arbuzova—a somewhat dark, gypsylike lady, of the ballerina type; Yegor Konstantinovich Yarkin—thirty-two years of age, non-Party, head of the First Municipal Bakery; and, finally, the stationmaster, Comrade Peter Pavlovich Sitnikov, respected by all.

The reader will also encounter a handful of peripheral personae, such as Yekaterina Vasilyevna Kolenkorova, Aunt Pepelyukha, and the station guard and Hero of Labor[1] Yeremeyich—but there's really no sense in discussing them in advance, considering the insignificance of their roles.

In addition to these human characters the tale also features a small dog, about which, needless to say, there's nothing to say.

2

The Belokopytovs are an old, aristocratic, landowning family. At the time these events took place, however, they were fading away. In fact, there were only two Belokopytovs left: the father, Ivan Petrovich, and his offspring, Ivan Ivanovich.

The father, Ivan Petrovich, a very rich and respectable individual, was a somewhat odd, eccentric gentleman. He was slightly populist in his tendencies but enamored of Western ideas, and would either rail against peasants, calling them swine and human scum, or shut himself in his library to pore over the works of such authors as Jean-Jacques Rousseau, Voltaire, and Baudouin de Courtenay, admiring the freedom of their thought and the independence of their views.[2]

And yet, despite all this, Ivan Petrovich Belokopytov adored the quiet, peaceful country life. He loved raw milk, which he imbibed in staggering quantities, and he was fond of horse riding. Never a day passed that Ivan Petrovich didn't go out on horseback, so as to admire the beauty of nature or the babbling of one or another forest brook.

Belokopytov the elder died young, in the full flower of his activity. He was crushed by his own horse.

One clear summer day, Ivan Petrovich stood at his dining room window, fully dressed and prepared for his usual ride, waiting impatiently for his horse to be brought round. Looking dashingly handsome in his silver spurs, he stood at the window, testily brandishing his gold-handled riding crop. Meanwhile, his son, youthful Vanya Belokopytov, gamboled about him, prancing blithely and toying with the rowels of his father's spurs.

Come to think of it, young Belokopytov must have done the gamboling at a much younger age. He was past twenty the year his father died—already a mature young man, with fuzz on his upper lip.

No, he certainly couldn't have been gamboling that year. He was standing at his father's side, trying to persuade him not to go riding.

"Don't go, papa," urged the young Belokopytov, who was filled with foreboding.

But the dashing father simply twirled his mustache and waved the young man away, as if to say, if my number's up, so be it. He went down to give the tarrying groom a tongue-lashing.

He stormed into the yard, angrily leapt onto his horse's back, and, in a fit of extreme irritation and wrath, dug his spurs into its sides.

And this, it seems, was his undoing. The furious animal bolted and, about three miles from the estate, threw Belokopytov, smashing his skull against the rocks.

Young Belokopytov took the news of his father's death in stride. After first ordering that the horse in question be sold, he withdrew his decision, marched into the stable, and personally shot the animal, placing the revolver directly in its ear. Then he locked himself in the house and bitterly lamented his father's demise. Only several months later did he again take up his former pursuits. He was a student of Spanish, and, under the guidance of a seasoned instructor, translated the works of Spanish authors. Of course, one should note that he was also a student of Latin, always digging through old books and manuscripts.

Now Ivan Ivanovich was the sole heir to an enormous fortune. Someone else in his position might have chucked all that Spanish stuff, given his instructors the boot, packed up his grief, and taken to wine, women, what have you. Unfortunately, young Belokopytov wasn't that kind of man. His life went on just as before.

Always rich and secure, he didn't know the meaning of financial constraints and treated money with indifference and contempt. And having read his fill of liberal books, with his father's notes in the margins, he even came to disdain his vast fortune.

Catching wind of the elder Belokopytov's death, all sorts of aunties descended upon the estate from every corner of the globe, each hoping to get a piece of the pie. They flattered Ivan Ivanovich, kissed his hand, and marveled at his wise directives.

Then one day Ivan Ivanovich gathered all his relatives in the dining room and declared that he felt he had no right to his inherited fortune. He thought the very notion of "inheritance" was "utter nonsense," and believed that human beings ought to make their own way in the world. And so he, Ivan Ivanovich Belokopytov, being of sound mind and in full possession of his faculties, would renounce his property, on the condition that he himself could distribute it to various institutions and disadvantaged individuals of his choice.

His relations oohed and aahed in unison, marveling at Ivan Ivanovich's extraordinary generosity and suggesting that, in essence, they were precisely the disadvantaged individuals and institutions of which he had spoken. After allocating them nearly half his fortune, Ivan Ivanovich bid them a final farewell and set about liquidating the rest of his possessions.

He quickly sold his land for a song and gave away part of his household goods and cattle to the peasants, squandering the rest. Still possessed of a sizable fortune, he moved to the city, renting two little rooms from some simple folk to whom he had no connection.

Some distant relatives of his, who were then living in the city, took offense and broke off all contact with Ivan Ivanovich, finding his behavior to be harmful and dangerous to the life of the nobility.

Settling in the city, Ivan Ivanovich didn't alter his life or habits one bit. He continued to study Spanish, and, in his spare time, engaged in a wide variety of charity work.

Huge crowds of beggars besieged Ivan Ivanovich's apartment. Every manner of rogue, scoundrel, and confidence man lined up to plead for his help.

Refusing almost no one and, in addition, sacrificing large sums to various institutions, Ivan Ivanovich soon squandered half his remaining possessions. On top of that, he befriended a certain revolutionary group, supporting and helping them in every possible way. There was even talk that he had given the group nearly all the money he had left, but the author can neither confirm nor deny that rumor. In any case, Belokopytov was involved in one revolutionary cause.

The author, for his part, was then occupied with his poetic and familial affairs, and turned a somewhat blind eye to social developments, so certain details escaped him. That year the author was preparing his first little book of poems for publication, under the title *A Bouquet of Mignonette*. At the present time, of course, the author would hardly apply so wretched and sentimental a title to his poetic experiments. At the present time, he would attempt to bind his humble verses with some abstract philosophical idea and give the collection a fitting title—just as this tale is bound and titled with that enormous, significant word: "People." Alas, at that time, the author was young and inexperienced. Still, the book wasn't so bad. Printed on the finest art paper in three hundred copies, it sold out completely in just over four years, bringing its author a certain degree of celebrity among the citizens of his town.

No, not a bad little book.

But as to Ivan Ivanovich, he really did get tangled up in the course of events. In a fit of generosity, he gave a mink coat to some girl student who had been sentenced to exile.

That coat gave Ivan Ivanovich no end of trouble. He was placed under secret surveillance, suspected of having relations with revolutionaries.

Ivan Ivanovich, a nervous and impressionable man, was terribly anxious about being watched. He literally clutched his head, saying that he refused to remain in Russia, a country of semi-barbarians, where they stalked men as if they were beasts. He promised himself that he would soon sell everything off and go abroad as a political refugee, freeing his legs from this stagnant swamp.

Having made this decision, he began to liquidate his affairs in a hurry, worried that he might be captured, arrested, or denied the right to emigrate. Then, one cloudy autumn day, with his affairs ended and with only a little money left for living expenses, Ivan Ivanovich Belokopytov went abroad, cursing his fate and his generosity.

This departure took place in September 1910.

3

No one knows how Ivan Ivanovich lived abroad, what he did there.

Ivan Ivanovich himself never spoke of it, and the author won't risk spinning yarns about the alien way of life in those lands.

Of course, some experienced writer who has seen foreign parts with his own eyes would gladly lay it on thick, beguiling readers with two or three European tableaux featuring late-night bars, cabaret singers, and American billionaires.

Alas! The author has never traveled to any foreign parts, and European life remains a dark mystery to him.

Hence, with some regret and sadness, and even a degree of guilt before the reader, the author must skip over at least ten or eleven years of Ivan Ivanovich Belokopytov's life abroad, in order not to bungle up any minor details of those alien ways.

But the reader should calm himself. Nothing remarkable happened in our hero's life over those ten years. I mean, the man lived abroad, married a Russian ballet dancer . . . What else? Went completely broke, of course. And at the start of the revolution, he returned to Russia. That's the long and the short of it.

Of course, all this could have been laid out in a better, more attractive manner—but again, for the reasons mentioned above, the author leaves everything as it is. Let other writers make use of their beautiful verbiage. The author isn't a vain man—if this is how he wrote it, so be it. The author loses no sleep over the laurels of other famed writers.

And so, dear reader, there you have the whole story of Belokopytov's ten years abroad. Well, not exactly.

In those early years in Europe Ivan Ivanovich conceived of a book. He even put pen to paper, titling his opus *The Possibility of Revolution in Russia and the Caucasus*. But then the world war and revolution rendered his book unnecessary, nonsensical rubbish.

But Ivan Ivanovich wasn't too disappointed, and in the third or fourth year of the revolution he returned to Russia, to the town he'd left behind. At this point the author picks up his tale. Here the author is in his element, completely in command. No chance of bungling it now. This isn't Europe for you. Everything here transpired before the author's own eyes. Every detail, every incident was either witnessed by the author directly, or was relayed to him by the most reliable of first hands.

And so the author begins his detailed account only from the date of Ivan Ivanovich's arrival in our dear city.

It was a lovely spring. The snow had almost completely melted away. Birds glided through the air, welcoming the long-awaited season with their cries. Yet it was still too soon to go about without galoshes; in certain places, the mud came up to the knees or higher.

On one such lovely spring day, Ivan Ivanovich Belokopytov returned to his native region.

It was the afternoon.

Several passengers were rushing from side to side on the platform, impatiently awaiting the train. Near them stood the stationmaster, Comrade Sitnikov, respected by all.

And when the train arrived, a slender man in a soft hat and pointed-toe boots without galoshes emerged from the front car.

That man was Ivan Ivanovich Belokopytov.

Dressed in European fashion, in an excellent broad coat, he casually stepped onto the platform after first tossing down two beautiful suitcases of yellowish leather with nickel-plated locks. Then he turned back and gave his hand to a somewhat dark, gypsy-like lady, helping her off the train.

They stood beside their suitcases. She kept glancing about with some dismay, while he simply smiled softly and breathed deeply, gazing at the departing train.

The train had long since moved away—but they stood motionless. A gang of feral urchins, whistling and slapping the platform with their bare feet, pounced on the suitcases. They pulled at the leather with their dirty paws and offered to drag them as far as the ends of the earth, if need be.

The porter and old Hero of Labor, Yeremeich, drove the boys off and began to eye the now-sullied pale-yellow suitcases reproachfully. Then, hoisting them on his shoulders, Yeremeich moved toward the exit, thereby suggesting that the newly arrived pair follow him and not just stand there like idiots.

Belokopytov followed him, but at the exit, on the porch behind the station, he ordered Yeremeich to stop. He himself stopped, took off his hat, and saluted his hometown, his country, and his return.

Standing on the steps of the station and smiling softly, he gazed at the street that ran off into the distance, at the gutters with their little bridges, and at the little wooden houses with the gray smoke rising from their chimneys . . . There was a certain quiet joy, a certain salutatory delight on his face.

He stood there a long time with his head uncovered. The mild spring breeze ruffled his slightly graying hair. Reflecting on his wanderings and on the new life that lay before him, Belokopytov stood motionless, drawing the fresh air deep into his chest.

And suddenly he wanted, that very moment, to go somewhere, do something, create something—something important and necessary to all. He felt an extraordinary surge of youthful freshness and strength welling up inside him, along with some kind of delight. And he wanted to bow low to his native land, to his hometown, and to all of mankind.

Meanwhile, his wife, Nina Osipovna Arbuzova, stood behind him, glaring nastily at his figure and impatiently tapping the cobblestones with the tip of her umbrella. A bit farther off stood Yeremeich, bent under the two bags, not knowing whether to put them on the ground and thus soil their dazzling surfaces, or to keep them on his back and wait for the command to move on. But then Ivan Ivanovitch turned to Yeremeich and kindly directed him to unburden himself—setting the bags down in the mud, if necessary. Ivan Ivanovich even walked up to Yeremeich and helped him lower the bags to the ground himself, saying:

"Well, how are things? How's life?"

Somewhat crude and utterly unimaginative Yeremeich, who wasn't accustomed to fielding such abstract questions and who had carried as many as fifteen thousand suitcases, baskets, and bindles on his back, replied rather plainly and crudely:

"Ain't dead yet . . ."

At that point Belokopytov began to question Yremeich about things and events more firmly rooted in reality, enquiring where this or that person now was, and what changes had occurred in town. But Yeremeich, who had lived in this town continuously for fifty-six years, didn't seem to recognize any of the names Belokopytov mentioned, be they of people or streets.

Blowing his nose and wiping his sweaty face with his sleeve, Yeremeich would first pick up the bags, as if to indicate that it was time to go, then put them back down, worrying that he'd be late to greet the next train.

Nina Osipovna broke into their friendly conversation, asking nastily whether Ivan Ivanovich intended to stay and live right there, in the bosom of nature, or whether he had something else in mind.

As she spoke, Nina Osipovna angrily tapped her shoe against the steps and dolefully pursed her lips.

Ivan Ivanovich was about to respond in some way, but then Comrade Peter Pavlovich Sitnikov, respected by all, emerged from his office. He had heard the hubbub and was accompanied by an agent of the criminal investigation division. However, seeing that all was well, and that the public peace and quiet had in no way been disturbed, and that, in fact, nothing at all had happened, aside from a family dispute involving the tapping of a lady's shoe against the steps, Peter Pavlovich Sitnikov began to turn back—but then Ivan Ivanovich ran up to him and asked whether he remembered him, gripping him firmly by the hand, shaking it, and rejoicing.

Maintaining his dignity, Sitnikov answered that he did indeed remember something, vaguely, and that there was something familiar about Belokopytov's countenance, but he could not say or recall anything definitively.

Pleading official business and shaking Belokopytov's hand, he withdrew, giving a wave to the unfamiliar dark woman.

The agent left as well, after first asking Belokopytov about international politics and events in Germany. He silently listened to Belokopytov's speech, gave a nod, and walked off, commanding Yeremeich to move the bags as far as possible from the entrance, so that passengers wouldn't break their legs.

Yeremeich irately shouldered the bags for the final time and started walking, asking where he ought to take them.

"Indeed," Nina Osipovna asked Belokopytov. "Where were you planning on going?"

With a certain degree of perplexity and concern, Ivan Ivanovich began to think about where he could go, but he simply didn't know, and so he asked Yeremeich whether there was a room available somewhere in the vicinity, if only on a temporary basis.

Lowering the bags once more, Yeremeich also began to think and try to remember. He finally concluded there was nowhere to go besides Katerina Vasilyevna Kolenkorova's, and so off he went. But Ivan Ivanovich ran ahead of him, saying that he remembered that most gentle woman Katerina Vasilyevna full well, and remembered full well where she lived, and that he would lead the way.

On he marched, his hands swinging at his sides and his exquisite foreign boots squishing in the mud.

Behind him trudged the completely exhausted Yeremeich. And behind Yeremeich walked Nina Osipovna Arbuzova, holding her skirt high and exposing her skinny, gray-stockinged legs.

4

The Belokopytovs took a room at Katerina Vasilyevna Kolenkorova's place.

Katerina Vasilyevna was a simple-hearted, kindly old woman, who was, for some strange reason, interested in anything other than political events.

She welcomed the Belokopytovs warmly, saying that she would assign them the very finest room in the house, right next to that of Comrade Yarkin, head of the First State Bakery.

And she led them to that room with a certain air of solemnity.

With some trepidation, inhaling the familiar odor of old provincial housing, Ivan Ivanovich entered a plain wooden mudroom, with many holes in the walls, a clay washing jug hanging from a rope in the corner, and a pile of rubbish on the floor.

Ivan Ivanovich walked through the mudroom with a kind of rapture, curiously examining the clay washing jug, the likes of which he hadn't seen in years, and proceeded inside. He liked everything about the place right away—the creaking of the floorboards, the thin partitions between the rooms, the dingy little windows, the low ceilings. He liked his room, too, although it was, in fact, not very good—the author would even say disgusting. And yet, for some reason, Nina Osipovna herself seemed to respond favorably to the room, opining that, as far as temporary arrangements went, it was perfectly reasonable.

The author attributes this exclusively to the couple's exhaustion. In later years, he had occasion to spend a good deal of time in this room, and he has never seen so tasteless a setup—although he himself lives in rather poor conditions, renting a room from people of modest means. With all due respect to the couple, the author is shocked at their taste. There was nothing the least bit attractive about their room. Its yellow wallpaper was peeling off and warping. Its meager furnishings consisted of a plain kitchen table covered with oilcloth, a few chairs, a couch, and a bed. And its only adornment, as it were, was a pair of antlers hung high on the wall. But you can't get very far on antlers alone.

And so, the Belokopytovs temporarily settled at Katerina Vasilyevna Kolenkorova's.

They immediately developed a quiet, measured routine. For the first few days they remained indoors, owing to the mud and terrible road conditions. They spent their time tidying up, admiring the antlers, and sharing their impressions.

Ivan Ivanovich was in a cheerful, jocular mood. He would run up to the window to marvel at some heifer or silly chicken pecking at the rubbish in the street, or race into the mudroom and, laughing like a child, splash about under the wash jug, dousing his hands first from one spout, then from the other.

Nina Osipovna—a delicate, coquettish individual—did not share her husband's enthusiasm for the clay jug. She would smile squeamishly and comment that she, in any case, preferred a real washstand—you know, the kind with a leg or foot pedal: you press it and water comes out. However, she expressed no specific grievances about the jug. On the contrary, she would often say:

"If it's only temporary, I'm perfectly fine with it—no complaints. A bad bush is better than an open field."

After her morning wash, Nina Osipovna's face would look pink, fresh, ten years younger, and she would hurry happily into the room.

There she would put on her ballet costume—those panties, you know, with the gauze skirt—and do her exercises before a mirror, squatting gracefully first on one foot, then on the other, then on both at the same time.

Ivan Ivanovich would gaze tenderly at her—at her trifling undertakings—finding, at the same time, that the provincial air had had a positively favorable effect on his wife. She had grown plumper, and her legs were no longer as skinny as they had been in Berlin.

Tired out by her squats, Nina Osipovna would plop down in some armchair or other, and Ivan Ivanovich would stroke her hand gently, telling her of his former life in these parts, of how he had fled eleven years earlier, pursued by the tsarist gendarmes, and of how he had spent his first years in exile. Nina Osipovna would ask her husband many questions, showing a lively interest in the extent of his former wealth and property. Shocked and horrified at how quickly and rashly he had squandered his fortune, she would reproach him angrily and sharply for his foolish carelessness and eccentricity.

"How could you? How could you throw money to the wind like that?" she would say, holding back her indignation.

Ivan Ivanovich would shrug his shoulders and try to change the subject.

Sometimes Katerina Vasilyevna would interrupt their conversations. She would enter the room, stand near the door, and, swaying from side to side, relay the latest gossip and tell them about all sorts of changes in town.

Ivan Ivanovich would question her eagerly about his distant relatives and few acquaintances. Learning that most of them had died, while others had gone abroad as political refugees, he would begin to pace the room anxiously, shaking his head. Eventually, Nina Osipovna would take him by the hand and sit him down on a chair, saying that he was getting on her nerves, flitting before her eyes like that.

So passed the first few days, without any worries, alarms, or incidents. Only once, in the evening, after knocking on their door, did their neighbor Yegor Konstantinovich Yarkin come into their room. After introducing himself, he spent a long time enquiring about life abroad, and in the end asked whether the suitcase standing in the corner was for sale.

Learning that the suitcase was not for sale but was just standing there for no good reason, Yegor Konstantinovich left the room, looking somewhat offended and bowing silently to its inhabitants.

Nina Osipovna stared squeamishly at his broad figure and bull-like neck as he exited the room, thinking dolefully that one was unlikely to find a truly refined gentleman in this provincial backwater.

5

Life proceeded on its usual course.

The mud dried a bit and people began bustling up and down the streets—some hurrying about their business, others simply promenading, cracking sunflower seeds, laughing, and peeping into other people's windows.

From time to time domestic animals would come out into the street and walk in front of the houses with measured steps, nibbling on some grass or pawing at the earth, so as to store up a little fat for the spring.

The highly educated Ivan Ivanovich, who was fluent in Spanish and knew enough Latin to get by, wasn't the least bit concerned about his prospects. He hoped that, in a few days' time, he would find appropriate employment and move to a new and better apartment. Talking the matter over with his wife, he would calmly explain that, although his financial circumstances were, at present, strained, the situation would soon improve. Nina Osipovna would beseech him to hurry up, get down to it, and determine where he stood. Ivan Ivanovich relented, promising to do so the very next day.

His first steps, however, did not meet with success. A bit discouraged, he went to some other establishments the following day, but returned glum and slightly agitated. Shrugging his shoulders, he made excuses. It wasn't as easy as all that, he explained to his wife— a man who knows Latin and Spanish isn't just handed a decent position.

Every morning he would go out looking for work, but he was always turned away—either because, these employers claimed, there was no suitable position, or because he had no relevant experience.

It should be said that Ivan Ivanovich was given a friendly and attentive reception everywhere he went. All the employers were endlessly curious about his experiences abroad and the possibility of new global shocks—but whenever the conversation turned to work, they would shake their heads and shrug. Their hands were tied, they'd explain, adding that Spanish, that rare and amusing language, was, unfortunately, not in particularly high demand.

Belokopytov stopped mentioning his Spanish. He now gave greater emphasis to his Latin, banking on its practical applications. But the Latin too fell on deaf ears. Employers were willing to hear him out—and they even took some interest in the Latin, asking him to recite some ditty or phrase, just for the sound of it—but they saw no practical application for it.

And so Ivan Ivanovich stopped emphasizing his Latin. He now looked for any kind of writing work, and would have settled for a job filing papers, but he was always asked about his skills and his professional experience. Upon hearing that Ivan Ivanovich had no skills or professional experience, employers would take offense, saying that it was wrong to waste busy people's time.

Here and there, Belokopytov was asked to stop by the following month, but he was given no concrete promises.

Ivan Ivanovich Belokopytov would now come home in a gloomy, depressed state. After a quick, rather lean dinner, he would collapse on the bed in his trousers and turn to face the wall, hoping to avoid any sort of conversation or row with his wife.

Meanwhile, she'd be jumping around in front of the mirror in her panties and pink gauze like a complete idiot, stamping her feet and throwing her skinny arms in the air, her sharp elbows flying every which way.

Sometimes she would try to start a row, heaping all sorts of unpleasant business on Ivan Ivanovich's head, and expressing her indignation at the fact that he had brought her here, from abroad, to live such a dull, insipid life. But Ivan Ivanovich, feeling and knowing himself to be guilty, kept silent. Only once did he respond, saying that he didn't understand a thing, and that he himself had been deluded about the Spanish language and about his whole life. He had counted on getting a decent position, but everything kept falling through—because, as it turned out, he was completely unskilled, unable to do anything. This had simply never occurred to him before. It turned out he had received a foolish and senseless upbringing, preparing him for the rich, prosperous life of a landowner and master of the house. And now, when he had nothing to his name—he was reaping that upbringing's rewards.

Nina Osipovna burst into tears, saying that things couldn't go on this way, that something had to give—after all, they owed money to everyone, even to their dear old landlady, Katerina Vasilyevna. Then, asking her not to cry, Ivan Ivanovich suggested that she sell the suitcase, even if they had to sell it to their neighbor Yegor Konstantinovich Yarkin.

And that is precisely what she did. She personally took the suitcase to Yarkin's room, sat there for a long time, and returned with money in hand and a new spring in her step.

From that point on there were no more rows. Or rather, whenever Ivan Ivanovich anticipated a row, he would put on his hat and go out into the street. And every time he passed through the mudroom, he would hear his neighbor Yegor Konstantinovich talking to Nina Osipovna through the wall, offering her a piece of bread or a cheese sandwich.

Ivan Ivanovich would walk through the gate and stand in the ditch by the side of the road, staring sadly down the long street. Sometimes he would sit perfectly still on a bench near the front garden, hugging his knees and glancing anxiously at the passersby.

People would walk down the street, hurrying about their business. Some old woman carrying a basket or a bag would examine Ivan Ivanovich curiously, then move on, looking back ten or fifteen times. A gang of little boys would run past, sticking out their tongues or slapping him on the knee and scurrying off.

Ivan Ivanovich observed all this with a sad smile, reflecting for the hundredth time on one and the same thing—on his own life in comparison with those of others, trying to isolate some kind of difference or some terrible reason for his unhappiness.

Every once in a while a group of workers from the textile factory would saunter past Belokopytov with their harmonica, jokes, and songs. And then Belokopytov would perk up and gaze at them for a long time, listening to their loud, joyous songs, shouts, and cheers.

And on those days—those days of sitting in the ditch—it seemed to Ivan Ivanovich that he shouldn't have come to this town, to this street. But where should he have gone instead? He had no idea. And so he would make his way home, more worried and stooped than before, dragging his feet along the ground.

6

Ivan Ivanovich lost heart altogether. The ecstasy he had felt upon arrival now gave way to silent anguish and apathy.

He was somehow frightened of life, about which, it turned out, he knew nothing. It now seemed to him that life was some kind of deadly struggle for the right to exist. And so—in mortal anguish, sensing that the very continuation of his life was at stake—he sifted through his store of knowledge and abilities, as well as the means of applying them. Unfortunately, after poring over everything he knew, he came to the sad conclusion that he knew nothing. He spoke Spanish, played the harp, had some familiarity with electricity and could, for example, install an electric bell—but here, in this town, all those skills appeared to be unnecessary, and were even regarded as somewhat odd and amusing. No one laughed in his face, but he would receive smiles of sympathy, as well as sly, mocking glances; and then he would cower, walk away, and try to avoid people.

By sheer force of habit, he still went out every day, at the usual hour, to look for work. Steadily, trying to walk as slowly as possible, he would, just as before, utter his requests in an almost mechanical manner, without the slightest trepidation. He would be told to come back in a month, and was at times simply and curtly denied.

On some occasions, when he was driven to dull despair, Ivan Ivanovich would reproach people angrily, demanding work and assistance posthaste, laying out his services to the state and telling the story of the more-or-less mink coat he had given to the exiled girl student.

He would drag himself around town all day long, and toward evening, half-starved and grimacing, he would wander aimlessly from street to street, house to house, trying to delay, to put off returning home.

Now and then he would cover the whole town on foot, simply going and going without halting anywhere. Passing the outskirts, he would find himself in the open field, cross the "Dog's Grove," and walk into the woods, where he would wander around until dusk and only then return home.

He would enter his room with his eyes closed, knowing that Nina Osipovna was sitting motionless to his left, near the mirror, staring at him nastily or through tears.

He avoided conversation, avoided seeing her at all, staying in the house as little as possible and only at night.

But one day he himself broke the silence.

He said that everything had gone to hell, that he was turning himself over to the hands of fate, and that she, Nina Osipovna, could, if necessary, dispose of his property as she saw fit. What he had in mind was the remaining suitcase and a few items of his foreign wardrobe.

Catching wind of this through the thin partition, Yegor Konstantinovich Yarkin walked into the couple's room and announced that he was happy to meet their wishes, but categorically refused to purchase the suitcase.

"Suitcases—nothing but suitcases," Yegor Konstantinovich complained. "Don't you have anything else to offer?"

Learning that they had, he began to examine certain items, including a pair of trousers, bringing them close to his eyes. Peering at the trousers against the light, he found fault with them, denigrating their quality.

Nina Osipovna—enlivened and, for some reason, excited—joked with Yegor Konstantinovich, slapping him lightly on the hand or sitting gracefully on the arm of his chair and shaking her skinny leg.

In the end, Yegor Konstantinovich politely bid them good day and stepped out, taking the items of clothing and leaving a sum of money.

The next few days were calm and quiet. But at the end of that week, Ivan Ivanovich, who had left the house early in the morning, returned at noon, quite shaken and aglow. He had found a job. This whole time he had been looking for some kind of silly intellectual writing work, but it turned out there were other options!

At any rate, he happened to run into an old friend in the street. After solicitously inquiring about and learning of Ivan Ivanovich's maddening situation, the man clutched at his head, pondering what he could do to help his comrade as quickly as possible. Somewhat abashed, he said that he could, at least temporarily, set Ivan Ivanovich up at one of the consumer cooperatives.

But this would only be temporary—for an individual as erudite as Ivan Ivanovich required a position suitable to his stature.

Ivan Ivanovich leapt at the offer with unrestrained joy, saying that he accepted the job sight unseen, that this sort of work was positively to his liking, and that he wouldn't want any sort of problematic changes. After agreeing to everything, Ivan Ivanovich dashed home. There, tugging at Katerina Vasilyevna's and his wife's hands, he spoke breathlessly about his new position.

Quickly, right on the spot, he laid out a whole philosophical system concerning the need to adapt—concerning the straightforward, primitive nature of life, and the fact that every person, endowed with the right to live, is obliged, like any living thing, like any animal, to alter his or her spots with the changing times. What need had he of stupid intellectual work? Here was a wonderful profession, which would furnish him with a new zest for life! Who needs all that Spanish, all those sophisticated minds, and so on.

Babbling in confused, garbled sentences, breaking off in the middle of words and jumping from thought to thought, he sought to prove his theory. Nina Osipovna listened to him without understanding a thing, nervously smoking cigarette after cigarette.

The author surmises that Ivan Ivanovich Belokopytov, knocked slightly off balance by strong emotions, had in mind that great scientific theory of protective coloration—of so-called mimicry—in accordance with which a bug crawling on a stem has the same color as the stem, so that some bird doesn't peck at him, having taken him for a breadcrumb.

This is all perfectly clear and understandable to the author. Yet he isn't the least bit surprised that Nina Osipovna couldn't make heads or tails of it. The author doesn't hold ballet dancers in particularly high esteem.

7

Ivan Ivanovich Belokopytov enrolled in "The Public Good" cooperative.

He would now get up at the crack of dawn, put on his suit—which was by then quite shabby—and, trying not to wake his wife, tiptoe out of the house and hurry to work. He was almost always the first at the door, and would often have to stand there for an hour or more, waiting for the manager to arrive and open the shop. He was also last to leave the shop, along with the manager. He would hurry home, jumping over ditches, carrying whatever eatables he had been issued under his arm.

Back home, babbling breathlessly and interrupting himself, he would tell his wife that the new job was very much to his liking, that he wanted nothing else from life, that being a shop clerk wasn't so very shameful and humiliating, and that, in the grand scheme of things, the job was quite pleasant and not too difficult.

Nina Osipovna reacted to this change in Ivan Ivanovich's life rather sympathetically, saying that if this arrangement were merely temporary then it wasn't as bad as it might seem at first glance, and that in the future they might even be able to open a humble little cooperative of their own. Developing on this notion, Nina Osipovna would go into utter rapture, conjuring a picture of them doing trade: him behind the counter, strong, with his sleeves rolled up and a cleaver in his hand, and herself—graceful, lightly powdered—at the cash register. Yes, she would stand at the register, smile cheerfully at the customers, and count the money, binding the bills into neat little packets. She loved to count money. Even the dirtiest of bills was cleaner than any apron and stack of dishes.

With these thoughts in her head, Nina Osipovna would clap her hands, slip on her pink tights and gauze, and commence her idiotic jumping and curtseying. Meanwhile, Ivan Ivanovich, exhausted by a long day's work, would tumble into bed and drift off, eagerly looking forward to the morning.

The following day, returning from work, Ivan Ivanovich would share his new experiences with his wife. He would laugh as he told her of how, say, he had weighed some butter—and of how a barely noticeable application of one finger to the scale radically changes an object's weight, to the considerable advantage of the clerk.

Nina Osipovna would perk up at those moments. She would wonder why Ivan Ivanovich had only applied one finger to the scale, rather than two, saying that two would have reduced the butter's weight still further. She also deeply regretted that he hadn't swapped the butter for some worthless yellowish muck, maybe clay.

Ivan Ivanovich would laugh off his wife's suggestions and beg her not to interfere in his affairs, so as not to go too far over the edge and thus cause him to lose the job. But Nina Osipovna would angrily advise him not to be excessively tenderhearted and dewy-eyed in his practices.

Ivan Ivanovich agreed. He would declare—getting a bit worked up—that cynicism was an absolutely necessary and normal quality, that no beast could get along without cynicism and cruelty, and that, in fact, cynicism and cruelty may be the most proper qualities of all, since they secure the right to live. Ivan Ivanovich would also proclaim that he had once been a foolish, sentimental puppy, but that he had now grown up and understood what it cost to live. He had even realized that his former ideals—compassion, generosity, morality—weren't worth a rusty kopeck and a rotten egg. They were all pathetic trifles belonging to a false, sentimental era.

Nina Osipovna had no patience for such abstract philosophical ideas. She would peevishly wave her hand, saying that she entirely preferred concrete, visible facts and money to all his words.

And so the days passed.

Ivan Ivanovich Belokopytov managed to make several purchases and acquisitions. For instance, he bought a few soup plates with blue rims, two or three pots, and, finally, a kerosene stove.

The purchase of the kerosene stove was cause for celebration—a real moment of triumph. Ivan Ivanovich unpacked it with his own hands and showed Nina Osipovna how to operate it, how to cook lunch and warm up meat.

Ivan Ivanovich became the master of his home and a prudent man. He now deeply regretted having let his neighbor have all his foreign suits for a song. But he would console himself right away, saying that it was only a matter of time—and not much time— before he could buy a good, plain suit, of a color that wouldn't show dirt.

Alas, Ivan Ivanovich never did get to buy that suit.

One day Ivan Ivanovich left the shop before closing time and, having shoved two pounds of stearin candles and a piece of soap into his briefcase, walked through the courtyard toward the street.

He was stopped at the gate by a guard, who demanded to examine the contents of his briefcase.

Ivan Ivanovich, who suddenly looked rather haggard, stood perfectly still, staring silently at the guard. The guard said he had received strict orders not to let anyone out of the yard without a search, and repeated his demand.

Ivan Ivanovich was completely stunned, and found it hard to understand what was happening. He allowed the guard to open the briefcase. To the joyful shouts of the crowd, the guard extracted the ill-begotten candles and soap.

Belokopytov was invited to the station. The candles were confiscated and he was interrogated. After drawing up a damning report, the guards released him, poking fun at his comic appearance—mocking this figure with the empty, unbuttoned briefcase pressed to its chest.

It all happened so quickly and unexpectedly that Ivan Ivanovich staggered out into the street without a clear sense of his position. At first he set off for home, but then turned left before reaching Saint-Just Street and walked on in a rather odd manner, without moving his hands or head.

He kept going for a few blocks, sat on some little bench for a while, then returned home late at night.

Entering the house, he groped his way through the dark like a blind man, made his way to his room, and lay down on the bed. Turning to the wall, he began to trace the pattern on the wallpaper with his fingers.

He didn't breathe a word to his wife. Nor did she ask any questions, having already learned of the day's events. Yegor Konstantinovich had brought her the news after returning from work.

And now, despite Belokopytov's presence, Yegor Konstantinovich rapped lightly on the wall and asked Nina Osipovna whether she needed anything, whether she'd fancy a glass of tea and a sandwich.

Without so much as glancing at her husband, Nina Osipovna replied in a chesty, melodious voice that she was stuffed to the gills and was going to bed. Yegor Konstantinovich asked something else, courteously and politely, but she responded, undressing and yawning, that she was asleep.

And she did indeed lie down on the couch. Covering her face with her hands, she lay there strangely, without moving a muscle. Ivan Ivanovich got up to put out the light, but, after looking at the sofa, sat down and stared at his wife for a long time. It seemed to him that she was in a desperate state, close to death. And he wanted to go over to her, kneel down, and say something in a calm, cheerful tone. But he couldn't bring himself to do it.

8

He stretched out in bed, trying not to move or think. But he couldn't help thinking—not about what had happened earlier in the day, but about his wife, about her unhappy life, and about the fact that not everyone had the right to exist.

Thinking these thoughts, he began to drift off. Some sort of terrible fatigue fettered his legs, and some sort of weight pressed down on his whole body.

He closed his eyes and lay perfectly still. His breathing grew steady and calm.

But then a cautious shuffling of feet and the creak of the door startled him awake.

He opened his eyes with a shudder, sat up in bed, and gazed around the room nervously. The small kerosene stove was barely burning, casting a few meager long shadows. Ivan Ivanovich looked at the couch—his wife was gone.

Worried and anxious, he jumped to his feet and carefully walked across the room on tiptoes.

Then he ran to the door, opened it, and—frightened, shivering, his teeth chattering in the predawn hours—rushed into the corridor. He dashed into the kitchen and took a quick look in the mudroom. All was quiet and calm—except for the chicken in the mudroom, who was spooked by Ivan Ivanovich and jumped away with a terrible cry.

Belokopytov returned to the kitchen. Katerina Vasilyevna was now sitting up in her bed, yawning and making little signs of the cross over her mouth. She was listening close to the unusual noise. Catching sight of Ivan Ivanovich, she lay down again, assuming that he had gotten up to answer nature's call.

But Ivan Ivanovich came up to her and began to tug at her hand, begging her to tell him whether his wife had passed through the kitchen.

Making signs of the cross and shrugging her shoulders, Katerina Vasilyevna pled ignorance. Then she began putting on her skirt, saying that if Nina Osipovna had stepped out, well, she'd likely be back.

Once Katerina Vasilyevna was dressed, she walked up to tenant Yarkin's locked door and told Ivan Ivanovich that his wife hadn't left the house. If she wasn't in the Belokopytovs' room—well, he might want to try the neighbor's.

Beckoning Belokopytov with her finger, she led him into the corridor and up to Yarkin's door, where she put her eye to the keyhole.

Ivan Ivanovich also wanted to approach the door, but at that moment the floor beneath him creaked, and he heard a bustle in the neighbor's room. Yegor Konstantinovich himself came up to the door, his bare feet slapping across the floorboards, and asked hoarsely: "Who's there? Whaddaya want?"

Ivan Ivanovich wanted to remain silent, but instead he said: "It's me . . . Is Nina Osipovna Arbuzova . . . with you, by any chance?"

"That's right," Yarkin answered rudely. "Whaddaya want?"

Receiving no reply, he grabbed the door handle.

A broken whisper sounded in the room. Nina Osipovna was pleading with Yarkin, begging him to hand over some revolver, saying that everything would be fine, just fine. Then she herself approached the door and took hold of the handle, asking softly: "Vanya . . . Is that you?"

Ivan Ivanovich winced, muttered something vague, then slunk away to his room. There, he sat down on the bed.

The author speculates that Ivan Ivanovich felt no particular despair. Sure, he might have sat down on the bed with evident despair, but that despair only lasted a moment. Once he had the chance to turn it over in his mind, he was probably even delighted.

Indeed, the author can't imagine why Ivan Ivanovich wouldn't be delighted. A terrible burden had been lifted from his shoulders. After all, Nina Osipovna's life had been his constant concern; he had had to provide her with all sorts of entertainment, theater, the best piece of bread. Now that Ivan Ivanovich's life had deteriorated so dramatically, feeding a little lady of this sort would be all the more difficult. After jumping all day in front of the mirror, the woman ate enough for two.

And so, after sitting on the bed a little while longer and reaching the conclusion that he had nothing to worry about, Ivan Ivanovich stretched out again. He lay there until morning, without closing his eyes. He wasn't thinking of anything, but his head buzzed and felt as if it were full of lead.

When Ivan Ivanovich got up the next morning, he was a rather different Ivan Ivanovich. The sunken eyes, the sallow, wrinkled skin, the tousled hair—it was an extraordinary change. And even after he had washed up with cold water, the change refused to disappear.

Ivan Ivanovich dressed, combed his hair out of habit, and left the house. He slowly made his way to the cooperative, but suddenly turned aside sharply, winced, and walked away.

On he plodded, step after step—dully, mechanically. Reaching the edge of town, he set off for his favorite spot in the woods, past the "Dog's Grove."

He crossed the grove, treading on yellow autumn leaves, and walked out into the clearing.

The whole clearing was pitted with old wartime trenches, dugouts, and bunkers. Scraps of rusty barbed wire hung from small stakes in the ground.

Ivan Ivanovich loved this place. He had often wandered through the trenches, lain at the edge of the woods, and smiled slyly to himself as he gazed at all these military ventures. But now he crossed the clearing somewhat indifferently, as if he noticed nothing. When he reached the woods, he sat down on a half-collapsed dugout, which had been built maybe seven years earlier.

He sat there for a long while, thinking of nothing, then walked farther, and then came back again and lay down on the grass. He lay with his face down for a long time, pulling at the grass with his hands. Then he got up and went back to town.

It was early autumn. Yellow leaves littered the ground. And the earth was warm and dry.

9

Ivan Ivanovich was now living alone.

Returning home after his wanderings and glumly surveying his barren lodgings, Ivan Ivanovich would sit on his bed, tallying the objects that had vanished along with Nina Osipovna. The number of such objects was, it turned out, nothing to sneeze at: gone were the kerosene stove bought in happier days, the tablecloth, and even the mirror and the small bedside rug.

Ivan Ivanovich wasn't so very troubled by these losses. "To hell with them!" kind Ivan Ivanovich thought, listening to the chatter on the other side of the wall.

The chatter was all whispers; it was impossible to make out any words. From time to time, he would hear the bass notes of Yegor Konstantinovich. In all likelihood, Yegor Konstantinovich was consoling Nina Osipovna, who was anxious to maintain her new well-being and retain the objects she had taken without her husband's permission.

But Ivan Ivanovich couldn't care less about objects. Every morning he would walk to the edge of town, go past the grove and the clearing, and approach the woods.

There he would sit on his dugout or roam the woods, tripping over tree roots, thinking about, or rather, contemplating his new position. He tried to capture what had befallen him—what had happened, why it had happened—in some single thought.

His wife had left him. She had no choice but to leave. He was a man of the old world, unfit for the struggle. Women follow the victor. Well, there it was—clear as day. And now nothing would save him from certain death.

Death was certain. He knew that, but by force of some sort of will he still tried to find a way out—to come up, at least theoretically, with some possible way out, some possible means of prolonging his existence. He didn't want to die. On the contrary, whenever the idea occurred to him, he would drive it from his mind, dismissing it as absurd and useless. At such moments, he would try to think of something else.

Roaming the woods, Ivan Ivanovich would ask himself why he shouldn't just make his home right there. He pictured himself living in the half-collapsed dugout, surrounded by mud and dirt, and crawling out on all fours, like an animal, in search of food.

He would laugh it off, of course.

But now he no longer returned home every evening. Sometimes he would stay in the woods. Half-starved, greedily chewing on raw mushrooms, roots, and berries, he would fall asleep under some tree, his hands folded under his head.

If it rained, he would crawl into the dugout. Crouching and hugging his skinny legs, he would listen to the raindrops beating against the trees.

10

It was autumn. The rains never ceased. Once again, it was impossible to go out without galoshes. Once again, the mud came up to one's knees.

Nina Osipovna's life with Yegor Konstantinovich Yarkin was quiet and carefree. Her exercises in dance had to be laid aside. She was pregnant, and Yegor Konstantinovich, fearing for his posterity, strictly forbade her from dressing up in all that frilly pink rubbish, threatening to burn the rags in the stove if she resisted. After a bit of capriciousness and a few tears, she resigned herself. Now she just sat beside the window, staring blankly at the muddy street. From time to time she would ask Yarkin whether he'd heard anything about her husband. Yegor Konstantinovich would just smile and wave his hand, telling her to avoid thinking about her husband for the sake of their child.

And Nina Osipovna would fall silent, but would still wonder why she heard fewer and fewer footsteps in the next room.

Indeed, Ivan Ivanovich came home less and less, and when he did return to town, he avoided meeting people. Whenever he encountered anyone, he would run across the street, looking terribly embarrassed and trying to hide his soggy, browned suit.

Ivan Ivanovich no longer even set foot in his room. Coming home, he would stop in the mudroom and silently greet Katerina Vasilyevna, always afraid that she might holler, stamp her feet, and chase him away. But Katerina Vasilyevna—never hiding her surprise and pity, and, for some reason, never even inviting him into the kitchen—would bring out a piece of bread, some soup, or whatever was left after dinner. Without so much as trying to hold back her tears, she would cry as she watched Ivan Ivanovich tear at the food with his thin, gray fingers and swallow it, smacking his lips and gnashing his teeth.

After eating everything that had been brought to him and grabbing another piece of bread, Ivan Ivanovich would touch Katerina Vasilyevna's sleeve and run off again.

He would return to his dugout. There he would sit in his customary position, coughing and spitting on his suit.

But he hadn't lost his mind, this Ivan Ivanovich Belokopytov. The author has reliable information on his meeting with one of his old friends. At this meeting, Ivan Ivanovich spoke about his life in a perfectly rational and even somewhat ironic manner. Shaking the rags of his foreign suit, he laughed loudly, saying that it was all nonsense, that a person shed his possessions—shed everything—as an animal sheds its skin in the fall.

Bidding his friend farewell with a firm handshake, he retreated into his dugout.

Ivan Ivanovich's new life was strange and hard to understand. He tried to think of nothing and to live just for the sake of living, with no special purpose, but it appears he couldn't help but think, turning his various plans over in his mind. Each time he came to the conclusion that life in the dugout wasn't so terribly bad, but that, of all the animals, he was the very worst, with his chronic bronchitis and runny nose. Coming to this conclusion, Ivan Ivanovich would nod sadly.

The thought of certain death now occurred to him ever more frequently, but, just as before, he would reject the idea of suicide with some vexation. It seemed to him that he had neither the will nor the desire to kill himself, and that not a single animal had ever perished by its own hand.

Was this due to the weakness of Ivan Ivanovich's will, or some vague hope? Impossible to say. At any rate, one day, quite suddenly, Ivan Ivanovich came up with a plan by which he would perish without resorting to self-inflicted violence.

It happened early in the morning. The autumn sun was still below the trees when Ivan Ivanovich awoke with a start in his dugout. It was dreadfully damp. Shivers and chills ran through his whole body. He woke up, opened his eyes, and, all at once, had a perfectly lucid thought about his death. It seemed to him that he had to die that very day. He didn't know how or why—and he began to think. Suddenly it came to him: he would die like an animal, in some desperate struggle.

Scenes of this struggle began to take shape in his imagination. He saw himself locked in combat with another man, perhaps even Yegor Konstantinovich, for whom his wife had left him. They were biting each other, rolling in the dirt, pressing each other down, tearing at each other's hair . . .

Ivan Ivanovich was now wide awake. Trembling all over, he sat on the ground. He contemplated the plan carefully, thought by thought, trying not to miss a single detail.

Here he was, entering the room. He opens the door. Yarkin is sure to be sitting at the table to the right. Nina Osipovna would be sitting at the window, her hands folded on her stomach. Ivan Ivanovich would walk over to Yarkin and shove him, one hand hitting the shoulder, the other his chest. Yarkin would fall backward, banging his head against the wall. Then he would jump up, draw his revolver, and shoot his opponent—Ivan Ivanovich Belokopytov.

Once the plan was complete, Ivan Ivanovich leapt to his feet, but, hitting his head on the ceiling, got back down and crawled out of the dugout.

He set out for town at a calm, steady pace, methodically contemplating the details of his plan. But then, wanting to get it over with quickly, in one fell swoop, he took off running, kicking up dirt, leaves, and splashes of mud.

He ran for a long time—almost all the way home. It was only when the house was in sight that he slowed down, proceeding very quietly.

A little white mutt barked at him indifferently.

Ivan Ivanovich bent over, picked up a stone, and launched it with great precision.

The dog squealed and scurried behind a gate, then stuck out its snout and barked fiercely, baring its teeth.

Ivan Ivanovich grabbed a lump of dirt and aimed it at the dog. Then he launched another lump. And then he approached the gate and began to tease the animal with his foot, hopping up and down and trying to kick it in the teeth.

Some kind of rabid fury and fright took hold of the dog. It whined in mortal fear, raising its upper lip and trying to seize the human foot. But, again and again, Ivan Ivanovich managed to pull the foot away deftly, in the nick of time, smacking the animal with his hand or with yet another lump of dirt.

Aunt Pepelyukha ran out of the house as if scalded by boiling water, selecting the most terrible, violent expressions for the foul urchins teasing her dog. But when she saw the large, shaggy man, she gasped. At first she managed to say that a mature citizen ought to be ashamed of himself, teasing dogs like that. But then she again fell silent and stood motionless, her mouth agape, staring at the extraordinary scene before her.

Ivan Ivanovich, now on his knees, was waging battle against the little mutt, trying to tear its jaws asunder with his hands. The dog wheezed frantically, its paws scraping the ground.

Aunt Pepelyukha let out a strange, piercing shriek, ran up to Ivan Ivanovich, barely managed to snatch the dog from his hands, and hurried back into the house.

Ivan Ivanovich wiped his hands, which were bitten all over, and walked on, stepping slowly and heavily.

In describing this incident, the author falls prey to rather strange, unusual feelings. In fact, he is slightly upset by Ivan Ivanovich's act. Needless to say, the author hasn't the least bit of sympathy for the Pepelyukha mutt, may it go to the dogs—but he is upset by the uncertainty and absurdity of Ivan Ivanovich's act. He doesn't know for a fact whether, at that moment, Ivan Ivanovich had actually gone off his rocker—or whether he hadn't gone off his rocker. Was the whole thing only a game, an accidental occurrence, an extreme case of nerves? Anyhow, this is all terribly unclear and psychologically incomprehensible.

And mind you, dear readers—this lack of clarity concerns a personage intimately familiar and well known to the author! Now, imagine if the author had gotten mixed up with an unfamiliar character? Why, he'd start fudging it, he'd lie his head off!

Even the famed English author Jack London—he'd lie his head off too. The rumors about this incident were just too damned contradictory.[3]

Aunt Pepelyukha, for instance, swore up and down that Ivan Ivanovich was stark raving mad, drooling, his tongue hanging out of his mouth. Katerina Vasilyevna, no less devout a lady, was, broadly speaking, in agreement. Yet the station guard and Hero of Labor Yeremeyich held the opposite view. He insisted that Ivan Ivanovich Belokopytov was fit as a bull, and that the real sickos and loonies are usually put in special homes. Yegor Konstantinovich Yarkin, too, had every confidence that Belokopytov was in full possession of his faculties. As for respected Comrade Sitnikov, well, he wasn't about to weigh in on the matter, saying that, in case of dire need, he could contact a certain psychiatrist in Moscow. But that would drag out indefinitely and, anyway, was far from a sure thing. By the time Comrade Sitnikov got around to writing, and by the time the Moscow psychiatrist got around to replying—no doubt after a few stiff ones . . . And even though he's a Moscow psychiatrist, he might dish out such a load of nonsense . . . If you go and print it, just try and prove you had nothing to do with it. The author had better leave the whole business to the reader's own conscience and simply move on.

11

Ivan Ivanovich wiped his hands on his suit and proceeded to the house. Blood dripped slowly from his dog-bitten fingers, but Ivan Ivanovich, noticing nothing and feeling no pain, kept going.

He paused for a moment at the gate, cast a backward glance, then slipped into the yard. He dashed up the steps, opened the door, and quietly entered the mudroom.

A strange quiver ran through his body. His heart was pounding and his breathing was ragged.

He stood in the mudroom awhile, then went into the corridor, unobserved. Crossing the creaking floorboards, he approached Yarkin's room and stopped, listening close.

As usual, everything was quiet.

Ivan Ivanovich suddenly pushed at the door, flinging it wide open, and stepped over the threshold.

The scene was exactly as Ivan Ivanovich had imagined it. Yarkin sat at the table to the right. Nina Osipovna, her hands folded on her stomach, sat in an armchair to the left, near the window. There were glasses on the table, some bread. And a kettle was boiling on the hissing kerosene stove.

Ivan Ivanovich somehow took all this in at a single glance, and, continuing to stand still, gazed at his wife.

She gasped quietly when she saw him and sat up in her chair. But Yegor Konstantinovich waved his hands at her, begging her to stay calm for the sake of their child. Then, after rising to approach his guest, he stopped and sat down again, gesturing for Ivan Ivanovich to enter the room and close the door, so as not to lower the temperature in vain.

And Ivan Ivanovich entered. Slightly lowering his head and raising his shoulders, he walked up to the seated Yegor Konstantinovich and stopped two paces away from him. A deadly pallor suddenly spread across Yegor Konstantinovich's face. He sat in his chair, leaning back a bit, and moved his lips without budging.

For a few seconds, Ivan Ivanovich stood silent. Then, after quickly glancing at Yarkin—at the very spot he was supposed to strike—he suddenly smiled, stepped aside, and sat down on one of the chairs.

Yegor Konstantinovich now sat up straight and leveled his vexed, angry gaze on Belokopytov. Ivan Ivanovich, for his part, sat with his hands hanging limp, staring invisibly at some point in space. He was reflecting on the fact that he harbored neither anger nor hatred against this man. He could not and did not want to approach Yegor Konstantinovich and strike him. And so he sat there, feeling tired and ill. He didn't want anything. The only thing he wanted was a bit of hot tea.

Thinking these thoughts, he looked at the kerosene stove, at the kettle on the stove, and at the sliced bread. The lid on the kettle rattled, lifted by billowing steam, and water came boiling over, hissing on the kerosene stove.

Yegor Konstantinovich rose and put out the fire.

And then the room grew completely silent.

Seeing that Ivan Ivanovich was gazing fixedly at the kerosene stove, Nina Osipovna sat up in her chair once more and, dolefully pursing her lips, began to insist in a plaintive tone that she had no intention of keeping the stove for herself—she had only borrowed it, knowing that Ivan Ivanovich had no use for the thing.

But Yegor Konstantinovich waved his hands and begged her not to worry. In a calm, even voice, he told Ivan Ivanovich that he would never take the thing for free—that he would pay him the very next day, in full, at the market price.

"I would pay you today," Yegor Konstantinovich said, "but I haven't got the change. Be sure to stop by tomorrow morning."

"All right," Ivan Ivanovich replied curtly. "I'll stop by."

Then, all of a sudden, Ivan Ivanovich grew anxious, shifting in his seat, and turned to his wife, saying that he was terribly sorry for sitting there like that, covered in dirt, but he was just so tired.

She nodded, looking nervous and dolefully pursing her lips. Sitting up in her chair once again, she said:

"Vanya, don't be angry . . ."

"I'm not angry," Ivan Ivanovich answered plainly.

He rose to his feet and moved one step closer to his wife, then bowed and left the room without saying a word, quietly closing the door behind him.

He went out into the corridor, stood there a moment, and then started for the front door.

Katerina Vasilyevna was waiting for him in the kitchen. Afraid, for some reason, to utter a word, she beckoned him over with gestures, inviting him to have a seat and eat some soup. Ivan Ivanovich—also, for some reason, not saying a word—shook his head, smiled, patted the landlady on her hand, and left the house.

Katerina Vasilyevna ran out after him with a cry, but Ivan Ivanovich turned and waved his hand, indicating that he didn't wish to be followed, and disappeared through the gate.

12

Ivan Ivanovich didn't return for the stove money. He vanished from town.

Yegor Konstantinovich Yarkin ran through the streets in search of Ivan Ivanovich, stopping at every establishment, money in hand. He kept insisting that he had nothing to do with it, that the money was for the stove—here it was, the money—that he had no desire to use someone else's goods, and that, if he didn't find Ivan Ivanovich, he would donate the money to an orphanage.

Yegor Konstantinovich even made it as far as the clearing, past the "Dog's Grove," but he never found Ivan Ivanovich.

Like a beast embarrassed to leave its dead body in plain view, Ivan Ivanovich vanished from town.

Comrade Peter Pavlovich Sitnikov and the station guard, Hero of Labor Yeremeyich, unanimously asserted that they had seen Ivan Ivanovich Belokopytov jump onto a departing train. But why had he jumped? Where had he gone? No one knew. He was never heard from again.

13

It was a lovely spring.

The snow had already melted away, and the birds were welcoming their new year. On one such day, Nina Osipovna Arbuzova brought forth her gift to the world, a beautiful boy of eight and a half pounds.

Yegor Konstantinovich was remarkably happy and satisfied.

The stove money—twelve gold rubles—did indeed go to the orphanage.

April 1924

A TERRIBLE NIGHT

1

You write and you write, but what're you writing for? Nobody knows.

I can just see the reader grinning. What about the money, I hear him say. Eh, you son of a gun? They pay you money, don't they? These writers sure do run to fat . . .

Oh, dear reader! What is money? So they pay you some money— so you go and buy some firewood, get your wife a pair of boots. And that's all. Money won't bring you peace of mind, won't give you any universal idea.

And yet, if you took away that measly, sordid little payment, the author would chuck literature altogether. He'd quit writing and snap his quill pen to bloody smithereens, devil take it.

I mean it.

The reader these days, he's a rotten sort. He goes crazy for French and American romance novels, but contemporary Russian literature? Wouldn't be caught dead with it. Today's reader, he wants sudden flights of fantasy—he wants some kind of plot, god only knows what kind.

But where's an author supposed to get all that stuff?

How can his fantasy suddenly soar when Russian reality won't comply?

And as for the revolution—well, that too is a tough spot. You've got your suddenness, alright. And you've got your majestic, grandiose fantasy. But just you try and write about it. They'll say you've bungled it. All wrong, they'll say. No scientificness of approach. And your ideology isn't so hot, either.

But where's the author supposed to get that approach? Where, I ask you, is the author supposed to get that scientific approach and ideology, if he was born in a petit bourgeois family and still can't suppress his sordid, philistine interest in money, flowers, curtains, and soft chairs?

Oh, dear reader! What a terribly uninteresting life we Russian writers lead.

A foreigner can write anything he wants—and it's water off a duck's back. He can write about the moon, let loose with sudden fantasy, talk all kinds of nonsense about wild beasts, or even send his hero to the moon in some kind of cannon ball . . .

Nothing will come of it.

But you just try and get away with that here. Try, for example, to send our technician Boris Petrovich Kuritsyn to the moon. They'll laugh at you. They'll take offense. Now you've gone and done it, they'll say, you dirty dog! What a load of bunk! Impossible!

So you write in complete awareness of your own backwardness.

As for glory, what glory? If you think about glory—again, what glory? Nobody knows what our descendants will make of our works, or what phase the earth will be in, geologically speaking.

In fact, the author recently read this one German philosopher who says that our whole life, the whole flowering of our culture, is nothing but an interglacial period.[1]

The author freely admits that a shiver ran through his body when he read that.

Really. Just imagine, dear reader . . . Abandon your daily concerns for a single moment and picture the following: there was, long before us, some kind of life and some kind of high culture, and then it vanished. Now you have a flowering again—but it too will vanish. Now, this might not affect us personally, but still . . . The melancholy sense of something fleeting, temporary, random, and constantly changing—it forces one to reconsider, time and again, one's own life.

Say you write a manuscript, breaking your head over the orthography, let alone the style. Then, in five hundred years' time, some mammoth comes along and stomps on it with his huge foot, riffles it with his tusk, gives it a sniff, and discards it as inedible rubbish.

There's no consolation in anything. Not in money, not in glory, not in honors. And on top of that, life is kind of funny—really rather poor.

You go out into the country, for example, out of town . . . You see a little house, a fence. Boring sight. There's a little cow standing out front, bored to tears . . . Manure on the side of her belly . . . She's shaking her tail . . . Chewing . . . You see a peasant woman sitting there, wearing some kind of gray kerchief. She's doing something with her hands. A rooster's walking back and forth. And everything, all around you, is poor, dirty, uncivilized . . .

Oh, what a boring sight!

And say an old peasant comes up to the woman. His hair's light brown. He's like a walking plant. He comes up and looks at her with his bright little eyes—like shiny marbles—wondering, what's the old woman doing? He hiccups, scratches one leg against the other, yawns. "Eh," he says, "I'm bored. Suppose I'll go and catch me some sleep. Not much else to do . . ." And off he goes.

And you want a sudden flight of fantasy!

Ah, gentlemen, gentle comrades! Where am I supposed to get a flight of fantasy? And how do I adapt fantasy to this country-side reality? Be so kind as to tell me—do me a favor! Really, I'd be happy to blow things out of proportion, so to speak—but I can't start from scratch.

And in town, where the lamps shine bright, where citizens walk back and forth in complete awareness of their human greatness—well, there too you won't always get the suddenness of fantasy.

So they walk back and forth, these citizens.

But if you follow one of them, reader—exert some effort and follow him—you'd be surprised at the nonsense he's up to.

Turns out he's off to borrow three rubles, or to meet with some woman or other. I mean, really!

He shows up, sits down in front of his lady, says something about love—or maybe he doesn't even say anything, just plants his hand on the lady's knee and looks into her eyes.

Or maybe he pays some other fellow a visit. He gulps down a cup of tea, takes a peek at himself in the samovar—thinks to himself, "Helluva mug," grins, spills some jam on the tablecloth, and leaves. That's right—just claps his hat onto the side of his head and leaves.

And if you ask the son of a bitch why he'd come in the first place, what universal idea informed his visit, what benefit it brought to mankind—why, he himself doesn't know.

Of course, in this case—in this boring depiction of urban life—the author focuses on minor, insignificant figures like himself, rather than on government officials, say, or on educators, who really do walk back and forth on important public business.

The author certainly didn't have such big shots in mind when he spoke of ladies' knees, for example, or even of crooked mugs in samovars. These important people may indeed be capable of thought, of suffering, of concern. They may want other people's lives to be more interesting. They may dream of a world with more room for sudden flights of fantasy.

The author, looking ahead in advance, rebuffs presumptuous critics who, out of sheer mischief, will charge him with distorting provincial reality and being unwilling to see the positive side.

The author is not distorting reality. He doesn't get paid for distortions, dear comrades.

Yes, there's no question about it: the author sees things as they are.

Take one urban fellow the author knew personally. He lived a quiet life—the kind of life almost everyone lives. He ate and drank, put his hands on his lady's knees and peered into her eyes, spilled jam on the tablecloth, and borrowed three rubles with no plans of giving them back.

The author's very short tale will concern this fellow. Perhaps it won't concern this fellow, exactly, but rather a foolish and insignificant adventure that cost the fellow twenty-five rubles in the course of legal collection. This happened very recently—in August 1923.

Should the author dilute the event with fantasy? Should he wrap it up in a diverting marital affair cut from whole cloth? No! Let the Frenchies have their fun—we'll go slow, step by step, on a par with Russian reality.

Of course, if the merry reader hungers for lively, sudden flights of fantasy and awaits juicy details and incidents—well, the author refers him, with a light heart, to foreign authors.

2

This short tale begins with a complete, detailed description of the entire life of Boris Ivanovich Kotofeyev.

Kotofeyev was a musician by trade. He played the musical triangle in a symphony orchestra.

This instrument may have a very special, particular name—the author doesn't know it. At any rate, the reader has likely glimpsed a stooping, somewhat slack-jawed individual sitting in front of a small steel triangle in the depths of the orchestra, off to the right. This fellow gives his uncomplicated instrument a sad little jangle at the appropriate moment. Typically, the conductor indicates the moment by winking his right eye.

There are so many strange, surprising professions in this world.

Some of these professions . . . One shudders to think how a man could arrive at them. How, for example, does a man decide to walk a tightrope, whistle through his nose, or jangle a triangle?

But the author isn't mocking his hero. Not at all. Boris Ivanovich Kotofeyev was a man possessed of a fine heart, intelligence, and a secondary education.

Boris Ivanovich didn't live in the center of town. He lived in the suburbs—in the bosom of nature, as it were.

This nature, of course, was no great shakes. However, the small gardens in front of the houses, the grass, the ditches, the wooden benches littered with sunflower seed shells—it all contributed to a pleasant, attractive atmosphere.

In springtime the place was just lovely.

Boris Ivanovich had a room at Lukerya Blokhina's house on Rear Avenue.

Imagine, dear reader, a small wooden house painted yellow, a low, rickety fence, and a wide yellow gate hanging crooked on its hinges. A yard. In the yard, to the right, a little shed. A rake with broken teeth that hasn't budged since the days of Catherine the Great. A cart wheel. A stone in the middle of the yard. A porch with its lower step torn off.

You get up on the porch and see a door upholstered in bast. Beyond that, you got your inner porch, half-dark, with a green barrel in the corner. A board on top of the barrel. A dipper on top of the board.

A water closet with a flimsy door—just three boards cobbled together. A little latch on the door. A piece of glass in place of a window. Cobwebs all over the glass.

Oh, familiar, heartwarming scene!

There was a certain charm to it all—the charm of a quiet, boring, placid life. To this day, the thought of that torn-off porch step, despite its intolerably sad appearance, still puts the author in a calm, contemplative mood.

But whenever Boris Ivanovich looked at that gnarled, torn-off step, he would shake his head and spit aside in disgust.

It was fifteen years ago that Boris Ivanovich Kotofeyev first set foot on this porch and first crossed the threshold of this house. He never did leave. He married his landlady, Lukerya Petrovna Blokhina, becoming lord and master of the entire estate.

The wheel, the shed, the rake, the stone—all these were now his inalienable property.

Lukerya Petrovna observed Boris Ivanovich's transformation into lord and master with a nervous grin.

In fits of anger, she'd shout and take Kotofeyev to task, saying that he himself was a pauper, without a thing to his name, spoiled by her many favors.

Hurt though he was, Boris Ivanovich would say nothing.

He had come to love this house—to love the yard with the stone. He had come to love living here during those fifteen years.

Some people—well, you can tell their whole story, describe their whole life, in ten minutes' time, from their first senseless cry to their last days on earth.

That's just what the author will try to do. Very briefly, in ten minutes' time, the author will try to tell the whole life story of Boris Ivanovich Kotofeyev, without omitting a single detail.

Actually, there's nothing to tell.

His life ran on, quiet and peaceful.

And if you chop this life up into periods, well, you'd get five or six little parts.

Here you have Boris Ivanovich beginning his life after graduating from trade school. Here you have him as a musician playing in an orchestra. Here's his affair with a chorus girl. Here's him marrying his landlady. The war. Then the revolution. And before that, the fire in the suburb.

It was all plain and simple, giving rise to no hesitation or doubt. Most importantly, none of it seemed accidental. To all appearances, it was exactly as it should be, happening, so to speak, in accordance with the outline of history.

Even the revolution, which at first confused Boris Ivanovich considerably, later turned out to be quite plain and simple in its firm insistence on definite, excellent, and very realistic ideas.

And everything else—his choice of profession, friendship, marriage, war—didn't seem to be merely fate's game of chance. No, it all appeared to be extraordinarily solid, firm, and unconditional.

Perhaps the only thing that to some degree shattered the orderly system of his firm and not at all accidental life was the love affair. Here, the situation was more complicated. Boris Ivanovich admitted that this particular episode was accidental and could very well not have occurred in his life. The fact is, at the beginning of his musical career, Boris Ivanovich Kotofeyev took up with a chorus girl from the Municipal Theater. She was a young, trim blonde with vague, pale eyes.

Boris Ivanovich was twenty-two back then, and still rather handsome. Perhaps the only thing that somewhat marred his appearance was a slack lower jaw. It lent his face a sad, bewildered expression. But his luxuriant upright whiskers concealed the annoying protrusion to a sufficient degree.

How did this love affair start? No one knows for sure. Boris Ivanovich always sat in the depths of the orchestra, and, in the early years, for fear of striking the instrument at the wrong time, never took his eyes off the conductor. So it's still unclear how he managed to wink at the chorus girl.

Of course, in those years, Boris Ivanovich enjoyed life to the fullest. Footloose and fancy free, he would stroll up and down the boulevard in the evenings and would even attend dance parties. Wearing the light-blue ribbon of a master of ceremonies, he would conduct the dances himself, fluttering about the hall like a butterfly.

It's quite possible that he made the chorus girl's acquaintance at one such party.

In any event, this acquaintance brought Boris Ivanovich no joy. The romance got off to a fine start, alright. Boris Ivanovich even went so far as to plan out his future life with this pretty little woman. But a month later the blonde suddenly broke off relations, after sarcastically mocking his unfortunate jaw.

Somewhat embarrassed by his beloved's carefree departure, Boris Ivanovich decided, after some thought, to trade in the life of a provincial lion and desperate paramour for a quieter mode of existence. He didn't like things that happened by chance, things that could change.

It was then that Boris Ivanovich moved out of town, renting a warm room with a table for a small fee.

And there he married his landlady. This marriage—accompanied by a house, an estate, and a measured life—brought total peace to his anxious heart.

A year after the marriage, there was a fire.

The fire destroyed nearly half the suburb.

Boris Ivanovich, drenched in sweat, personally dragged the furniture and quilts out of the house and placed them in the bushes.

But the house didn't burn down. The windows burst and the paint peeled, but that was all.

And in the morning, Boris Ivanovich, cheerful and radiant, dragged his belongings back inside.

That fire left quite a trace. For years on end, Boris Ivanovich would share his experiences with friends and neighbors. But that, too, has now faded away.

And so, if you close your eyes and think about the past, all of these things—the fire, the marriage, the revolution, the music, the light-blue ribbon of a master of ceremonies—they've all faded away, merging into one continuous straight line.

Even the amorous incident has now faded away, transforming into some sort of annoying recollection, a boring anecdote about how the chorus girl had asked for a patent leather handbag, and how Boris Ivanovich had put aside ruble after ruble, saving up the necessary sum.

That's how the man lived.

That's how he lived until the age of thirty-seven—until that very moment, that exceptional occurrence for which he was fined twenty-five rubles by the court. That was his life—all the way up to that very adventure for the sake of which the author has taken the risk of ruining a few sheets of paper and of draining a small phial of ink.

3

And so Boris Ivanovich Kotofeyev lived to the age of thirty-seven. In all likelihood, he'll live a good while longer. He's a hale man, strong and big-boned. As for the limp—which is, anyhow, hardly noticeable—that's just a sore foot. It dates back to the tsarist regime.

The foot didn't bother him any, and Boris Ivanovich led a good, measured life. There was nothing he couldn't handle, and nothing to give him pause. But then, in the last few years, Boris Ivanovich began to think. He suddenly felt that life wasn't as firm in its grandeur as he had assumed.

He was always afraid of chance and tried to avoid it, but now it seemed to him that life was lousy with chance. Many events in his own life now appeared to be purely accidental, having occurred for absurd, meaningless reasons that needn't have existed.

These thoughts troubled and frightened Boris Ivanovich.

Once, he even broached the subject in the company of his closest friends.

This happened at his own birthday party.

"It's all rather strange, gentlemen," Boris Ivanovich said. "Everything in our lives is somehow, you know, accidental. What I'm saying is—it all happens by chance . . . For example, my marriage to Lukerya . . . I'm not saying I'm dissatisfied—I'm not saying anything at all. But it happened by chance. I mean, I could have taken a room elsewhere. I turned down this street purely by chance . . . Does that— does that make this an accident?"

His friends grinned at each other crookedly, awaiting a domestic disturbance. But there was no disturbance. Lukerya Petrovna, keeping her composure, simply left the room in a pointed manner, drank a dipper of cold water, and came back to the table merry and refreshed. At night, however, she let him have it good and strong, so that the neighbors even tried to summon the fire department in order to tamp down the family strife.

But even after the strife Boris Ivanovich lay on the couch with his eyes open and continued to ponder his thought. He was thinking that not only his marriage, but also his playing the triangle and, in general, all his vocations were merely an accident, a mere concurrence of circumstances.

"And if it's all accidental," thought Boris Ivanovich, "then nothing is certain. There's no solidity to it. It can all change tomorrow."

The author has no desire to prove the correctness of Boris Ivanovich's contentious thoughts. But, at first glance, everything in our venerable life does indeed seem partly accidental. Our birth is accidental, our existence is accidental—composed as it is of accidental circumstances—and our death, too, is accidental. This forces one to contemplate the fact that there isn't a single strict, rigid law on earth that would protect our lives.

And indeed, what strict law could there be, when everything constantly changes, constantly wavers before our eyes, from the grandest of things to the most minor of human inventions?

For instance, many generations, and even entire remarkable peoples, had been brought up on the fact that god exists.

And now any more or less competent philosopher can easily, with one stroke of the pen, prove the opposite.

Or take science. Here everything might seem terribly convincing and certain, but you look back—and nothing is certain. It all changes, over and over again, from the earth's rotation to some theory of relativity or probability or what have you.

The author never received a higher education and is hard pressed for exact chronological dates and proper names, so he won't try to prove any of this in vain.

It would be especially vain since it's highly unlikely that Boris Ivanovich Kotofeyev actually thought about any of this. He was a clever enough fellow, and possessed of a secondary education, but he wasn't nearly as sophisticated as certain men of letters.

Still, he did perceive a kind of shrewd little pitfall in life. And at some point he even began to doubt the certainty of his fate.

One day this doubt broke out in flames.

That day, returning home down Rear Avenue, Boris Ivanovich Kotofeyev bumped into a dark, hatted figure.

The figure stopped in front of Boris Ivanovich and, in a frail voice, asked for help.

Boris Ivanovich reached into his pocket, drew out some change, and gave it to the beggar. Then he gave the beggar a closer look.

Suddenly embarrassed, the beggar shielded his throat with his hand, as if apologizing for the absence of a collar and tie. Then, in the same frail voice, he said that he was a former landowner—that he himself used to give beggars handfuls of silver, but now, thanks to the new democratic way of life, he was forced to ask for help, since the revolution had taken away his estate.

Boris Ivanovich began to question the beggar, taking a keen interest in the details of his former life.

"What can I say?" said the beggar, flattered by the attention. "I tell you, I was filthy rich, rolling in it—and now, well, you see I'm dead broke, starving. Eh, good citizen . . . how things change . . ."

Handing the beggar another coin, Boris Ivanovich quietly set off for home. He didn't really pity the man, but he was overcome by some sort of vague uneasiness.

"How things change," kind Boris Ivanovich kept muttering.

Back home, Boris Ivanovich told his wife, Lukerya Petrovna, all about the encounter. One must say that he exaggerated a bit, adding some touches of his own, such as his description of the landowner tossing gold at the beggars and even breaking a few noses with the weightier coins.

"So what?" asked the wife. "He used to live well, now he lives badly—nothing odd about that. You don't have to go far—our neighbor's in mighty bad shape, too."

And Lukerya Petrovna began to tell her husband about Ivan Semyonovich Kushakov, the former teacher of calligraphy who had fallen on hard times. He used to live pretty well himself, and even smoked cigars.

Kotofeyev somehow took this teacher close to heart, too. He began to ask his wife all about Kushakov's descent into poverty.

Boris Ivanovich even wanted to pay the teacher a visit. He wanted to take immediate action in regard to his awful life.

He begged his wife Lukerya Petrovna to go and fetch the teacher straightaway, so that they could treat him to tea.

After scolding her husband and calling him a "lout," just to keep up appearances, Lukerya Petrovna, devoured by curiosity, threw on her shawl and scarf and ran out to fetch the teacher.

The teacher, Ivan Semyonovich Kushakov, came almost immediately.

He was a gray-haired, dried-up little old man in a worn-out long coat with no vest. His dirty, collarless shirt was bunched up on his chest. And the lump of his yellow, terribly bright copper tiepin somehow flashed far out in front of him.

The graying stubble on the calligraphy teacher's cheeks had not been shaved for a long time and grew out in little shrubs.

The teacher entered the room, rubbing his hands and chewing on something as he walked. He bowed to Kotofeyev slowly, though almost gaily, and, for some reason, winked at him.

Then he sat down at the table, reached for a plate of raisin bread, put a piece in his mouth, and began to chew it, quietly chuckling to himself.

After the teacher had eaten his fill, Boris Ivanovich began to interrogate him with keen curiosity about his former life, asking how and why he had sunk so low, going about without a collar, in a dirty shirt, with one naked tiepin.

Rubbing his hands and winking gaily, though slyly, the teacher responded that he did indeed used to live pretty well and even smoked cigars, but, due to a shift in demand for calligraphy and by decree of the People's Commissars, the subject was stricken from the curriculum.

"But that's fine with me," said the teacher. "I've made my peace with it—no complaints. And I only ate your bread out of habit, not out of hunger."

Lukerya Petrovna sat there with her hands folded on her apron, laughing. She sensed that the teacher was stretching the truth and was about to snap it altogether. Staring at the teacher with undisguised curiosity, she awaited something completely out of the ordinary.

While Boris Ivanovich kept listening, shaking his head and muttering something.

"What can I say?" the teacher asked, again grinning for some unknown reason. "Things change. Today they get rid of calligraphy, tomorrow it's drawing, and then, before you know it, they'll come after you."

"Now wait, hold on a minute," Kotofeyev said, somewhat breathless. "After me? But I'm in the arts . . . I play the triangle."

"So what?" the teacher said scornfully. "Science and technology, they're going great guns these days. They'll think up an electric whatchamacallit—that there instrument—and it's the end of the road . . . Jig's up."

Kotofeyev, again somewhat breathless, looked at his wife.

"Man's right," his wife said. "If science and technology keep going . . ."

Boris Ivanovich suddenly rose and began pacing the room nervously.

"Alright, if that's how it is, so be it," he said. "So be it."

"Easy for you to say," his wife responded. "I'm the one footing the bill. You'll be a weight around my fool neck, Pilate-martyr."

The teacher fidgeted in his chair and said, in a conciliatory tone:

"That's how it goes: today it's calligraphy, tomorrow it's drawing . . . Everything changes, your lordships."

Boris Ivanovich approached the teacher and bade him farewell. After asking his guest to join them, at the very least, for dinner the following day, he offered to see him to the door.

The teacher rose and bowed. Stepping into the hallway, he repeated, gaily rubbing his hands:

"Don't you worry, young man—today calligraphy, tomorrow drawing, and then you'll get yours."

Boris Ivanovich closed the door behind Kotofeyev, went into the bedroom, sat down on the bed, and hugged his knees.

Lukerya Petrovna came into the room in worn felt slippers and began to tidy up for the night.

"Today it's calligraphy, tomorrow it's drawing," Boris Ivanovich kept muttering, swaying slightly on the bed. "That's life—our whole life."

Lukerya Petrovna glanced at her husband, furiously spat on the floor without saying a word, and began to untangle her matted hair, brushing out bits of straw and wood chips.

Boris Ivanovich looked up at his wife and suddenly spoke in a melancholy voice:

"Really, Luka, what if they do invent electronic percussion instruments? Imagine—a button on the music-stand . . . The conductor pokes it—and ding . . ."

"Oh, it's simple," said Lukerya Petrovna. "Clear as day . . . A weight around my neck . . . I can feel it already!"

Boris Ivanovich moved from the bed to a chair and sank into thought.

"Down in the dumps, are you?" Lukerya Petrovna asked. "Thinking, are you? Picking at your brain . . . Where would you be without a wife and home? Eh, you tramp? Say they drum you out of the orchestra?"

"The trouble isn't my getting drummed out, Luka," Boris Ivanovich said. "The trouble is that it's all wrong. Accidental... For some reason, Luka, I play the triangle. Just think... If they take that away from me, how would I live? What, besides the triangle, can I hold onto?"

Lukerya Petrovna lay in bed and listened to her husband, trying in vain to unravel the meaning of his words. Sensing in them an insult to her person and a claim to her property, she reiterated:

"A weight around my neck—I can feel it, you Pilate-martyr! Oh, you son of a bitch."

"I won't weigh you down," Kotofeyev said.

Breathless again, he rose from the chair and began pacing the room.

He was seized by terrible anxiety. Wiping his head with his hand, as if trying to brush off some vague thoughts, Boris Ivanovich again sat down in his chair.

And he stayed there, perfectly stationary, for a long time.

Later, when Lukerya Petrovna's breathing turned into a light snore with a faint whistle, Boris Ivanovich got up from his chair and left the room.

He found his hat, clapped it onto his head, and went out into the street in a state of some sort of extraordinary agitation.

4

It was only ten o'clock.

A lovely, quiet August evening.

Kotofeyev was walking along the avenue, swinging his arms wide.

He couldn't shake his strange, vague sense of anxiety.

Having paid no attention to where he was going, he found himself at the train station.

He ducked into the buffet, drank a glass of beer, and then, feeling breathless again, went out into the street.

Now he walked slowly, deep in thought, with his head sadly bowed. But if you were to ask him what he was thinking, he wouldn't tell you—he himself didn't know.

He kept moving away from the train station, then came to a mall near the city garden, sat down on a bench, and removed his hat.

A broad-hipped maiden in a short skirt and light-colored stockings passed by Kotofeyev once, then passed by him again, and then finally gave him a look and sat down on the bench.

Boris Ivanovich returned the girl's look, shuddered, shook his head, and quickly walked away.

And suddenly Kotofeyev felt that everything was terribly disgusting and intolerable. All of life seemed boring and stupid.

"What on earth was I living for?" Boris Ivanovich muttered. "I'll show up tomorrow and they'll tell me it's invented. They've got it, they'll say—they've got their electronic percussion instrument. Congratulations, they'll say. Go find another job."

A severe chill seized Boris Ivanovich's entire body. He walked faster now, almost at a run, then stopped when he reached the church fence. He fumbled with the gate, opened it, and went into the churchyard.

The cool air, the quiet birches, and the gravestones somehow calmed Kotofeyev immediately. He sat down on one of the stones and sank into thought. Then he said aloud:

"Today it's calligraphy, tomorrow it's drawing. That's life—our whole life."

Boris Ivanovich lit a cigarette and began to contemplate how he would live if something should happen.

"I'll go on, alright," Boris Ivanovich muttered. "But I won't go to Lukerya. I'd rather throw myself at the people's feet. Citizens, I'll say, before you, I'll say, is a dying man. Don't leave me in misery . . ."

Boris Ivanovich shuddered and rose to his feet. Tremors and chills seized his body once more.

Suddenly Boris Ivanovich got the idea that the electric triangle had been invented long ago—that they were keeping it hidden, like a terrible secret, so as to bring him down with a single blow.

Boris Ivanovich nearly ran out of the churchyard in some kind of anguish and quickly shuffled off down the street.

The street was quiet.

A few belated passersby were hurrying home.

Boris Ivanovich stood on the corner for a while, and then, almost without realizing what he was doing, approached a passerby, took off his hat, and said in a hollow voice:

"Citizen . . . Please help . . . A man might be dying before your eyes . . ."

The passerby gave Kotofeyev a frightened glance and quickly moved on.

"Ah!" Boris Ivanovich cried out, sitting down on the wooden sidewalk. "Citizens! Help me . . . In my misfortune . . . In my trouble . . . Give whatever you can!"

Several passersby surrounded Boris Ivanovich, staring at him in fear and bewilderment.

A policeman approached, anxiously patting his holster, and tugged at Boris Ivanovich's shoulder.

"He's drunk," someone in the crowd announced with pleasure. "Got a load on, the devil—and on a workday, too. Thinks he's above the law!"

The curious crowd surrounded Kotofeyev. A few compassionate fellows tried to lift him to his feet. Boris Ivanovich tore free from them and jumped aside. The crowd parted.

Boris Ivanovich looked about distractedly, gasped, and suddenly took off running without a word.

"Get 'im, boys! Grab 'im!" someone shrieked.

The policeman issued a shrill, piercing whistle. Its trill riled the whole street.

Boris Ivanovich didn't look back. He ran at a quick, even pace, keeping his head down.

People ran after him, whooping wildly, their feet slapping in the mud.

Boris Ivanovich rushed around the corner, reached the church fence, and jumped over it.

"That-a-way!" howled the same voice. "There he goes, brothers! Get 'im! Grab 'im . . ."

Boris Ivanovich ran up onto the church-porch, gasped quietly, glanced back, and leaned on the door.

The door gave way, creaking open on its rusty hinges.

Boris Ivanovich ran inside.

He stood motionless for a moment, then clutched his head and bounded up some rickety, dry, squeaky steps.

"That-a-way!" shouted the eager pursuer. "Get 'im, friends! Grab 'im any which way you can . . ."

Hundreds of passersby and townsfolk rushed through the fence and burst into the church. It was dark.

Then someone struck a match and lit a wax stub of a candle on a huge candlestick.

The bare high walls and the pitiful church plate were suddenly illuminated by a meager, flickering yellow light.

Boris Ivanovich was nowhere to be seen.

But just when the crowd, shoving and droning, began to rush back in some kind of fear, a booming tocsin sounded from the bell tower.

The chimes—at first sparse, then more and more frequent— swam through the quiet night air.

That was Boris Ivanovich Kotofeyev, swinging the heavy brass clapper with great effort and ringing the bell, as if deliberately trying to wake everyone in town.

This went on for a minute.

Then the familiar voice howled again:

"That-a-way! Can't let 'im run free, brothers! He's up there in the bell tower! Grab the bum!"

A few people rushed upstairs.

By the time Boris Ivanovich was taken out of the church, a huge crowd of half-dressed people, a police patrol, and the local fire squad had gathered at the fence.

Boris Ivanovich, supported under the arms, was led silently through the crowd and hauled off to the police station.

He was deathly pale and trembling all over, and his feet dragged disobediently along the pavement.

5

Subsequently, many days later, when someone would ask Boris Ivanovich why he had done all that—why, in particular, he had climbed into the tower and rung the bell—he would either shrug his shoulders and remain angrily silent or say that he didn't remember the details. And if someone should remind him of the details, he would wave his arms in embarrassment, pleading for them to stop.

On the night of the incident, Boris Ivanovich had been kept at the police station until morning. Then, after drawing up a vague, foggy report, they sent him home, under a pledge not to leave town.

Boris Ivanovich came home that morning, all limp and yellow— his coat ragged, his hat gone.

Lukerya Petrovna wailed loudly and pounded her chest, cursing the day of her birth and her whole miserable life with the human refuse that was Boris Ivanovich Kotofeyev.

But then, that very night, Boris Ivanovich was back in the depths of the orchestra, wearing, as usual, a clean, neat frock coat and giving his triangle sad little jangles.

Boris Ivanovich was, as usual, clean and kempt, and there was nothing to indicate the terrible night he had lived through.

It was only that two deep wrinkles now descended from his nose to the corners of his mouth.

Those wrinkles hadn't been there the previous day.

And the stoop in Boris Ivanovich's shoulders—that too was new.

But it'll all come out in the wash.

Boris Ivanovich Kotofeyev will live for a long time yet.

Hell, dear reader, he'll probably outlive us both.

1925

WHAT THE NIGHTINGALE SANG

1

I can just hear them laughing at us three hundred years from now! What strange lives, they'll say, these trifling folks lived. Running around with something called money, passports—registering so-called acts of social status, measuring out living space in square meters . . .

Well, let them laugh!

But one thing really gets my goat: the devils won't understand the half of it. And how could they? They'll be living the kind of life we've probably never even dreamed of!

The author doesn't know or wish to guess what kind of life they'll be living. Why rattle one's nerves and ruin one's health in vain? Chances are, the author won't even live to see this wondrous future life come to full flower.

And will it really be that wondrous, this future life? That's another question. For the sake of his own peace of mind, the author chooses to believe that this future life will be just as full of nonsense and rubbish as the one we're living.

On the other hand, the nonsense of the future could be real trifling stuff. For example—and excuse the author's poverty of thought—someone might spit on someone else's head from a zeppelin. Or maybe there's a mix-up at the crematorium, and instead of a dead relative, someone gets a perfect stranger's worthless dust . . . Nothing to be done about that, of course—you're bound to get petty troubles of that kind in the minor, day-to-day scheme of things. But the rest of life will probably be excellent, just terrific.

For all we know, there won't be any money at all. Everything'll be free, up for grabs. They'll be foisting all sorts of coats and scarves on all comers at the Arcade . . .

"Take it, citizen," they'll say. "It's a fine coat."

And you'll walk right past them. Your heart won't even flutter.

"Not a chance," you'll say. "To hell with your coat, dear comrades—I've got six already."

By gum, what a gay and appealing future life emerges before the author's eyes!

But this deserves deeper thought. If you toss out monetary considerations and selfish motives, what amazing forms this life might take! What excellent qualities human relationships might acquire! Love, for example. Why, this most exquisite of feelings might blossom forth in absolutely remarkable ways!

Oh, what a life—what a life it will be! The author contemplates it with such sweet joy, even though he remains an outsider, who hasn't the slightest guarantee of ever reaching it. But back to love.

Here the author must make a special comment. After all, many scientists and Party members generally dismiss the emotion of love. Excuse me, they say—what love? There's no such thing as love.

And there never has been. What you've got in mind, they say, is just another act of civil status—you know, like a funeral.

Here the author must disagree.

The author doesn't wish to confess to the casual reader, nor does he wish to disclose his intimate life to certain critics he finds particularly repulsive. Nevertheless, looking back on that intimate life, the author recalls a young maiden from the days of his youth. She had this sort of silly white face—tiny little hands, pitiful little shoulders. And yet the author would go into such sappy raptures at the very sight of her! What emotional moments the author would experience, when, out of an excess of all manner of noble feelings, he would fall to his knees and kiss the ground like an idiot.

Now that fifteen years have passed and the author has grown a little gray due to various illnesses, upheavals, and worries about his daily bread—now that the author simply doesn't wish to lie, and wishes, at long last, to see life as it is, without any falsehood or embellishment—he still insists, at the risk of appearing like a ridiculous person from the last century, that scientists and public figures are greatly mistaken.

Penning these lines about love, the author already anticipates a number of cruel retorts from public figures.

"Your own case," they'll say, "is no example, friend."

"What are you trying to prove," they'll say, "shoving your amorous intrigues in our faces?"

"Your personality," they'll say, "is out of step with our age, and, in general, has survived to the present day purely by chance."

You hear that? By chance! Forgive me, but what the hell do you mean, "by chance"? What would you have me do, throw myself under a tram?

"That's up to you," they'll say. "Under a tram, off a bridge . . . The point is, your existence is completely unjustified."

"Just look," they'll say, "at the simple, unsophisticated people all around you, and you'll see how differently they think."

Ha! You'll forgive the miserable little laugh, dear reader. Just the other day the author read in *Pravda* about a minor tradesman, a hairdresser's apprentice, who, out of jealousy, bit off a female citizen's nose.[1]

Well, if that isn't love, I don't know what is! I tell you, it's nothing to sneeze at. You think he bit off that nose to stimulate his palate? Well, to hell with you! The author doesn't wish to get upset and roil his blood. He still has to finish his tale, go to Moscow, and, on top of that, make a number of unpleasant visits to certain literary critics, asking them not to rush into print with all sorts of critical articles and reviews in connection to said tale.

And so, love.

People can think of this exquisite emotion however they wish. The author, recognizing his own insignificance and unfitness for life—and even acknowledging, devil take you, that there may be a tram in his future—holds fast to his opinion.

The author only wishes to inform the reader of a minor amorous episode that played out against the background of the present day.

"Again?" they'll ask. "Again with the minor episodes? Again with your petty trifles in a two-ruble book?"

"Young man," they'll say, "are you off your nut? Who needs all this stuff, in the cosmic scheme of things?"

The author pleads, honestly and openly:

"Don't interfere, comrades! Let a person speak his or her mind, at least in the course of debate . . ."

2

Boy, it sure is hard to write in the literary line!

By the time you fight your way through the impenetrable thickets, you're dog-tired, bled dry.

And for what? For the sake of some love story involving citizen Bylinkin. This fellow's neither kith nor kin to the author. The author's never borrowed a kopeck from him. Nor are he and the author bound by a common ideology. To tell the truth, the author regards the fellow with profound indifference. He has no desire to depict this Vasily Vasilyevich Bylinkin in vivid colors. What's more, the author doesn't even have a clear recollection of the man's face.

As for the others who took one or another part in this story, their faces too passed before the author's eyes without leaving much of an impression. The only exception is Liza Rundukova, whom the author committed to memory for very particular and, so to speak, subjective reasons.

Now Mishka Rundukov, her little squirt of a brother, was less memorable. He was an extremely cocky kid, and a bully. In terms of appearance, he was kind of tow-haired, a bit jowly.

In truth, the author doesn't really care to publicize the kid's appearance. He was in the age of transition. I'll waste time describing the kid—and by the time the book comes out, the little son of a bitch is all grown up. You just try and figure out who this Mishka Rundukov is. And where'd he get that mustache? At the time of this writing, there isn't a hair on his lip.

As regards the old woman—Ma Rundukova, as it were—well, I doubt the reader will mind us skirting her description altogether. Old ladies are, in general, difficult to describe artistically. She's an old lady, like any other. Who the hell knows or cares what kind of old lady she is? And who needs a description of, for instance, her nose? A nose like any other. Rest assured, dear reader—a detailed description of her nose won't make your life any easier.

Of course, the author would never have undertaken to write artistic tales were his information about the heroes limited to such meager and insignificant stuff. The author doesn't lack for information.

For example, the author has a vivid sense of the Rundukovs' entire existence. He can describe the wretched little Rundukov home—dark, single-story. On the façade, the number 22. Above that, on a little board, a picture of a pike hook. In case of fire. Everyone has to bring something. The Rundukovs, they have to bring a pike hook. But do they have a pike hook? I don't think so! Oh, well—it isn't literature's job to bring the county administration's attention to such matters.

And the whole interior of their little home—as well as, so to speak, its material design, in terms of furniture—emerges quite distinctly in the author's memory . . . Three small rooms. A warped floor. A Becker grand piano.[2] Terrible looking piano, but playable. A few sticks of furniture here and there. A sofa with a tomcat or pussycat on it. On the pier-glass table, a little clock under a glass dome. The dome's all dusty. And the pier-glass is clouded—twists your mug out of shape. A huge trunk, reeking of mothballs and dead flies.

Oh, I suppose a citizen from the capital would find their life mighty boring!

Oh, I suppose a citizen from the capital would be bored stiff at the sight of their clothes drying on a line in the kitchen. The old woman rustling up some food at the stove. Peeling potatoes, say. The peel curling away in ribbons from under the knife.

But the reader shouldn't think that the author describes these petty little things with love and admiration. No, sir! There isn't a hint of sweetness or romanticism in these petty recollections. The author knows these little houses, these kitchens. He's set foot in them. He's lived in them. Perhaps he even lives in one to this day. They have nothing to recommend them—absolutely pitiful. You walk into the kitchen and plant your face right into some wet underthing or other. And you're lucky if it's a relatively noble element of attire, rather than some wet stocking, Lord forgive me! Damn it, how the author hates planting his face in a stocking. Disgusting!

At any rate, for reasons wholly unrelated to literature, the author had several occasions to visit the Rundukovs. And on each of these occasions the author wondered how such an outstanding young lady—such a lily of the valley and nasturtium, so to speak—as Lizochka Rundukova could dwell amid all that pettiness and squalor.

The author always took great, great pity on this comely lass. We'll discuss her in detail and at length in due course. At this point the author must say a thing or two about citizen Vasily Vasilyevich Bylinkin—what kind of person he is, where he came from . . . Is he politically trustworthy? What has he to do with the respected Rundukovs? Is he a relative of theirs?

No, he's no relative. He just happened to get involved, temporarily, in their lives.

The author has already warned the reader that he didn't find this Bylinkin's countenance very memorable. All the same, closing his eyes, the author sees the man's every feature, lifelike as can be.

This Bylinkin always walked slowly, even thoughtfully. He held his hands behind his back and blinked an awful lot. His figure was somewhat stooped, apparently bent by circumstances. As for his heels, Bylinkin would wear them down to the very counters of his shoes.

With regard to education, he had spent, to all appearances, no fewer than four years at the old gymnasium.

Social origin unknown.

The man arrived from Moscow at the very height of the revolution and did not publicize himself.

Why had he come? Also unclear. Had life in the provinces seemed a bit more sated, as it were? Or could he simply not stay put, drawn as he was, so to speak, by unknown, far-flung places and adventures? The devil knows! You can't clamber into every psychology.

But most likely life in the provinces had seemed more sated. That's probably why, in the first few months, the man would walk through the open-air market and stare with relish at the fresh baked bread and all sorts of produce piled up in mounds.

Actually, how the man kept himself fed remains a vague mystery to the author. Perhaps he had even held out his hand. Or maybe he collected the corks from bottles of mineral water and fruit juice, and then sold them. Yes, the town had its share of desperate speculators in those days.

At any rate, the man clearly wasn't living too high on the hog. He was worn out, and even began to lose his hair. He walked timidly, glancing about and dragging his feet. He even stopped blinking and would simply stare at things wearily.

But then, for some unknown reason, his stock began to rise. And by the time our love story played out, Bylinkin had secured his social status, a position in the civil service, and a salary of the seventh category plus overtime.

Bylinkin's figure had filled out. He had reabsorbed, so to speak, the vital juices of which he'd been drained. He now blinked as frequently and casually as before.

He walked with the ponderous gait of a person whom life had hard-boiled, through and through—who had earned the right to live and knew his own worth.

Indeed, at the time these events unfolded, he was a fine figure of a man of just under thirty-two.

He often, time and again, promenaded the streets, swinging his walking stick wide and swatting flowers, grass, and even leaves along the way. Sometimes he would sit down on a bench and breathe deeply and cheerfully, with a broad smile on his face.

What he was thinking and what exceptional ideas embowered his head—no one knows. Perhaps he thought of nothing. Maybe he was simply filled with delight at his justified existence. But in all likelihood he was thinking about the absolutely necessity of finding a new apartment.

And it's true: he had been rooming at the house of Volosatov, a deacon at the Living Church, and, by virtue of his official position, was rather anxious about residing with such a politically sullied individual.[3]

He would ask all over town whether anyone knew, for god's sake, of some vacant little apartment or room, so that he wouldn't have to reside with the priest of what was obviously a cult.

At last, someone came forward and, out of the goodness of their heart, set him up with a small room—about four square meters. It happened to be a room in the house of the respected Rundukovs. Bylinkin leapt into action. He looked the place over that day, and moved in the very next morning, having hired, for said purpose, the water-carrier Nikita.

The father deacon didn't need this Bylinkin in his life, but the whole affair had apparently wounded his unclear yet refined feelings. He bawled Bylinkin out something awful, and even threatened to pound his face, given the chance. And when Bylinkin was loading his belongings onto the cart, the deacon stood at the window, laughing loudly and artificially, as though to demonstrate complete indifference to the man's departure.

The deacon's wife kept running out into the yard, throwing yet another item onto the cart and shouting:

"Good riddance! Who's stoppin' ya? Don't let the gate hit ya on the way out!"

A crowd of passersby and neighbors had gathered, guffawing with pleasure and clearly hinting at what appeared to be amorous relations. The author won't confirm their speculations. He doesn't know anything about it. And he certainly doesn't wish to start unnecessary gossip in the realm of belles lettres.

3

The decision to rent a room out to Vasily Vasilyevich Bylinkin wasn't motivated by self-interest, or even by any particular need. Rather, old Daria Vasilyevna Rundukova was afraid that, due to the housing crisis, their living space per person might be reduced with the forcible introduction of some crude and superfluous individual.

One might even say that Bylinkin took some advantage of this circumstance. Passing by the Becker grand, he cast an angry glance at the instrument and noted with displeasure that it was, generally speaking, superfluous; as a quiet man who had been rattled by life and shelled by artillery on two fronts, he could not tolerate superfluous bourgeois sounds.

The old woman took offense, saying that they had had their little grand for forty years now and weren't about to tear out its strings and pedals on some whim of Bylinkin's—especially since Lizochka Rundukova was learning to play the instrument, and this was quite possibly the girl's primary goal in life.

Bylinkin angrily waved the old woman away, saying that he had issued his statement in the form of a delicate request, not as a strict order.

The old woman was extremely offended. She burst into tears and almost rescinded her offer of the room, before she remembered the possibility of the forcible introduction.

Bylinkin moved in the next morning and groaned in his room till that evening, setting everything up in accordance with his capital-city taste.

Two or three days passed quietly, without much change.

Bylinkin would go to work, return late, and pace his room for a long time, his felt slippers shuffling across the floor. In the evening he would chew something and, at long last, fall asleep, snoring lightly and whistling through his nose.

During the first two days, Lizochka Rundukova went about somewhat subdued, repeatedly asking her ma, and also Mishka Rundukov, what they made of this Bylinkin—whether he smoked a pipe or bore any relation to the People's Commissariat of Naval Affairs.[4]

Finally, on the third day, she caught sight of Bylinkin with her own eyes.

It happened early in the morning. Bylinkin was getting ready for work, as usual.

He was walking down the corridor in his nightshirt, with his collar undone. His suspenders hung from his pants, fluttering behind him in various directions. He walked slowly, with a towel and a bar of scented soap in one hand. His other hand was smoothing down his hair, which had become disheveled in the night.

She was standing in the kitchen, busy with her domestic affairs, either fanning the samovar or chipping a bit of kindling off a dry log.

When she saw him she cried out softly and jumped aside, ashamed of her untidy morning attire.

While Bylinkin, standing in the doorway, regarded the young lady with a certain degree of surprise and delight.

It's true: that morning she looked very pretty indeed.

The youthful freshness of her slightly sleepy face, the careless cascade of her blond hair, the slightly upturned little nose . . . And the bright eyes. And the rather short but plump figure. All this was remarkably appealing.

She had about her the charming carelessness, perhaps even the slovenliness of the Russian woman who jumps out of bed in the morning, digs her bare feet into a pair of felt slippers, and busies herself with the housework without so much as washing up.

The author, you might say, likes such women. He certainly has nothing against them.

Of course, when you think about it, there's really nothing to recommend these heavy women with their lazy expressions. There's no liveliness in them, no brightness of temperament, and, finally, no flirtatiousness. A woman like that—she doesn't move much. Soft shoes, unkempt . . . Generally speaking, she's even a bit disgusting. But just imagine!

Dear reader, it's an odd thing!

The author has no time for those doll-like little ladies—those, so to speak, inventions of bourgeois Western culture. They've got these hairstyles—who knows what they are—Greek? Whatever they are, you can't touch them. And if you do, you'll hear no end of screaming and shouting. They've got these artificial dresses—and again, don't you dare touch. You might rip it, get it dirty. So tell me: who needs it? Where's the charm in all this, the joy of existence?

When one of ours sits down, for example, you see full well that the woman's sitting down. She isn't stuck on a pin, like one of theirs. That's what their women look like. Who needs it?

The author finds a lot to admire in foreign culture, but when it comes to women, he holds fast to his national opinion.

Bylinkin, too, it appears, was fond of such women.

In any case, he now stood before Lizochka Rundukova, mouth slightly agape with delight, and, without so much as trying to raise his dangling suspenders, stared at her in joyous surprise.

But this lasted only a minute.

Lizochka Rundukova, having gasped quietly and darted about the kitchen, now rushed out, adjusting her attire and tangled hair along the way.

When Bylinkin returned from work that evening, he walked to his room especially slowly, hoping to encounter Lizochka in the corridor.

But he did not.

Then, later in the evening, Bylinkin tramped to the kitchen five or six times and finally encountered Lizochka Rundukova, to whom he bowed with an awful degree of respect and courteousness, tilting his head slightly to the side and making that indeterminate gesture with his hands which conventionally indicates admiration and extreme pleasure.

A few days of such encounters in the corridor and kitchen brought them significantly closer.

Bylinkin would now come home, listen to Lizochka play this or that polka tremblam,[5] and beg her, again and again, to perform yet another heart-piercing composition.

And she would play some flea waltz or shimmy, or pound out a few bravura chords from the Second or Third, or, devil knows, perhaps even the Fourth of Liszt's Rhapsodies.[6]

And it was as if he, Bylinkin—who had been shelled by heavy artillery on all fronts twice—now heard the trembling strains of the Becker piano for the very first time. Back in his room, he would recline dreamily in his chair and ponder the charms of human existence.

Mishka Rundukov began to lead a very luxurious life. On two occasions Bylinkin slipped Mishka ten kopecks, and once gave him fifteen, asking him to whistle softly when the old woman was in the kitchen and Lizochka was alone.

The author can't quite imagine why Bylinkin would have done this. The old woman regarded the lovers with perfect delight, hoping to see them married no later than autumn, thereby getting Lizochka off her hands.

Nor did Mishka bother delving into the intricacies of Bylinkin's psychology. He simply whistled about six times a day, inviting Bylinkin to peer into this or that room.

Bylinkin would come into the room and sit down beside Lizochka. At first they would exchange a few meaningless phrases, then he would ask her to play one or another of her favorite ditties on the instrument. And there, at the grand piano, when Lizochka was finished, Bylinkin would place his gnarled fingers—the fingers of a philosophically minded man who had been hard-boiled by life and shelled by heavy artillery—on Lizochka's white hands. He would ask the young lady to tell him about her life, taking a lively interest in the details of her former existence.

Occasionally he would ask whether she had ever experienced the thrill of real, true love before, or whether this was her first time.

And the young lady, smiling mysteriously and quietly fingering the piano keys, would say:

"Oh, I don't know . . ."

4

They fell in passionate, dreamy love. They couldn't look at each other without tears and trembling. And every time they met they would experience new surges of rapturous joy.

In fact, when Bylinkin gazed into himself, he even took fright. He reflected with astonishment that, having twice spent time on all fronts and having earned, with extraordinary difficulty, the right to exist, he would now gladly sacrifice his life on any one of this rather pretty little lady's miserable whims.

Turning over in his mind the women who had passed through his life—including the deacon's wife, with whom he had most definitely cavorted (the author is sure of it)—Bylinkin grew convinced that he had found true love and the genuine thrill of emotion only now, in his thirty-second year.

Was Bylinkin merely bloated with vital juices? Or is a person born with a predisposition and penchant for abstract romantic feelings? This remains a mystery of nature.

At any rate, Bylinkin sensed that he was a different man now—that his blood had changed in its composition and that, when faced with a love of such extraordinary power, all of life was ridiculous and insignificant.

And Bylinkin—this slightly cynical man who had been hard-boiled by life and deafened by artillery, who had, on several occasions, come face to face with death—this terrible Bylinkin even developed a bit of a poetry habit, writing about a dozen verses of every kind and one ballad.

The author isn't familiar with his little rhymes, but one poem, entitled "To Her and This One," which had been submitted to *The Dictatorship of Labor* and rejected on the grounds of inconsonance with the socialist era, has accidentally—and by courtesy of the paper's technical secretary, Ivan Abramovich Krantz—fallen into the author's hands.

The author holds a dissenting opinion regarding verses and amateur poetry, and, hence, chooses not to trouble readers and typesetters by reproducing the longish poem in full. He will only draw the typesetters' attention to the final two stanzas, which are more sonorous than the rest:

I had referred to love as progress—
Such was the motto of my heart.

And I had eyes for nothing but
The image that your face imparts.
O Lizochka, yes, I have been
Reduced to ash within the fire
Of an acquaintance of this kind.

In terms of the formal method, these verses aren't so bad, I suppose. But, in general terms, they're pretty lousy stuff. They really are inconsonant and arrhythmic with our era.

Bylinkin didn't pursue poetry further, abandoning the poet's thorny path. Having always been somewhat prone to Americanism, he soon flung aside his literary achievements, buried his talent without regret, and went on with his former life, never again projecting his mad ideas onto paper.[7]

Bylinkin and Lizochka would now meet in the evenings, leave the house, and wander the deserted streets and boulevards late into the night. Sometimes they would go down to the river and sit on the sandy bluff, gazing at the swift waters of the river Kozyavka with deep and silent joy. At times they would hold each other's hands and gasp quietly, admiring the extraordinary beauty of nature or a light fluffy cloud racing across the sky.

All this was new to them, charming—and, most importantly, they felt they were seeing it all for the very first time.

Sometimes the lovers would walk past the town limits and go into the woods. There, holding each other's fingers, they would stroll all gentlelike. Stopping before some pine or fir tree, they would gaze upon it in astonishment, sincerely amazed by the bold and whimsical game of nature, which had flung up from beneath the ground a tree that was so necessary to mankind.

And then Vasily Bylinkin, shaken by the uniqueness of existence on earth and by its astonishing laws, would, out of an excess of emotions, fall to his knees before the young lady and kiss the soil around her feet.

And all about them—the moon, the mystery of the night, grass, fireflies chirping, the silence of the woods, the frogs and the bugs. All about them there was this sort of sweetness and serenity in the air. It's the joy of simple existence—a joy the author still refuses to reject wholeheartedly, which is why he cannot, under any circumstances, admit to being a superfluous figure against the background of the ascendant way of life.

And so, Bylinkin and Lizochka loved these walks past the town limits most of all.

But on one of these lovely walks, probably on a particularly damp night, the careless Bylinkin caught cold and fell ill. He came down with something on the order of mumps—or, as the doctors call it, epidemic parotitis.

By evening Bylinkin felt a slight chill and a stabbing pain in the throat. By night his mug was swollen something awful.

Lizochka would enter his room in soft slippers, weeping quietly, her hair down, and rush back and forth from bed to table, not knowing what to undertake, what to do, or how to ease the sick man's lot.

Ma Rundukova would also waddle into the room several times a day, asking the sick man whether he wanted cranberry jelly, which was, according to her, indispensable in fighting off any and all infectious diseases.

Two days later, when Bylinkin's mug swelled beyond recognition, Lizochka ran out to fetch a doctor.

After examining the sick man and prescribing some medicinal substances, the doctor left, likely cursing in his heart at having been summoned for such a trifle.

Lizochka Rundukova ran out after him. She stopped him in the street and, wringing her hands, began to babble, pleading: Well, how does it look? What's the verdict? Is there any hope? The doctor had got to know, she said, that she simply wouldn't survive this man's death.

At that point the doctor, who had grown accustomed to such scenes in his line of work, declared indifferently that mumps is mumps and, unfortunately, one needn't die of it.

Somewhat vexed by this insignificant danger, Lizochka glumly wended her way home and began to care for the sick man selflessly, sparing neither her meager strength nor her health—not even fearing to catch the mumps by way of infection.

In those first few days, Bylinkin was afraid to raise his head from the pillow. Probing his swollen throat with his fingers, he would ask in horror whether Lizochka Rundukova could still love him after this illness, which had enabled her to see him in such an ugly and disgusting state.

But the young lady begged him not to worry, saying that, in her opinion, he looked more dignified than ever before.

And Bylinkin would laugh, quietly and gratefully, saying that this illness sure had tested the fortitude of their love.

5

It was indeed an extraordinary love. And after Bylinkin's head and neck regained their former shape and he rose from his sick bed, he came to believe that Lizochka Rundukova had saved him from certain death.

This lent their amorous relations a degree of solemnity and even generosity.

One day, very soon after his illness, Bylinkin took Lizochka's hand and, adopting the tone of someone who had made a decision, begged her to hear him out without asking superfluous questions or interjecting with her silly remarks.

Bylinkin gave a long and solemn speech, declaring that he knew all about life and how hard it was to exist on earth, and that, in former days, when he was still a fledgling youngster, he had treated life with criminal nonchalance, for which he had paid dearly in his time, but that now experience had taught him how to live, had taught him the harsh and rigid laws of life. And finally he declared that now, after much deliberation, he had decided to introduce a change into the projected course of his life.

In short, Bylinkin made a formal proposal to Lizochka Rundukova, requesting that she not fret about her future well-being, even if she were henceforth unemployed and, therefore, unable to make a strong contribution to their modest communal pot.

Putting on a few airs and speaking briefly of free love—to accentuate the delicacy of the situation—Lizochka nevertheless enthusiastically accepted the proposal, saying that she had been waiting a long time, and that if Bylinkin hadn't popped the question, he'd be a complete louse and swindler. As for open relationships, well, they're well and good in their time, but this was a whole other kettle of fish.

Eager to share her joyous news, Lizochka Rundukova immediately ran to her mother, as well as to her neighbors, inviting them all to the wedding—a modest and intimate affair that would take place in the very near future.

The neighbors congratulated her warmly, saying that she had languished long enough as an old maid, tortured by the hopelessness of her existence.

Ma Rundukova shed a few tears, of course, and went to Bylinkin to ascertain the authenticity of the fact herself.

Bylinkin confirmed the old woman, solemnly asking for permission to refer to her, from that day forward, as "Ma." The old woman, crying and blowing her nose in her apron, said that she had lived on this planet for fifty-three years, but that this day was the happiest day of her life. She, in her turn, asked for permission to call Bylinkin "Vasya." Bylinkin graciously consented.

As regards Mishka Rundukov, well, Mishka took a rather indifferent attitude to the change in his sister's life, and was, at the present time, running around in the streets like a lunatic and sticking out his tongue.

Now the lovers no longer strolled past the town limits. For the most part, they sat at home and talked late into the night, planning out their future life.

And during one of these conversations Bylinkin, with pencil in hand, began to draft on paper a plan of their future rooms, which were to constitute a separate, small, but cozy apartment.

They argued with each other breathlessly as to where to put the bed, and where to put the table, and where to place the dressing table.

Bylinkin urged Lizochka not to be foolish enough to place the dressing table in the corner.

"How utterly provincial!" Bylinkin declared. "Placing a dressing table in the corner . . . Every young lady goes and does it that way. It's much better and more monumental to place a chest of drawers in the corner, and to cover it with a light lace tablecloth, which Ma, I hope, will not refuse us."

"A chest of drawers in the corner is just as provincial," Lizochka replied, almost in tears. "Besides, it's Ma's chest of drawers—who knows whether she'll give it to us."

"Nonsense," Bylinkin said. "How could she not give it to us? We can't keep our underthings on the windowsills, can we? Sheer nonsense."

"You should talk to Ma yourself, Vasya," Lizochka said sternly. "Talk to her as if she were your own ma. Tell her, 'Ma, dearest, give us that chest of drawers.' "

"Nonsense," Bylinkin said. "You know, if you'd like, I could go see the old woman this very minute."

And Bylinkin marched off to the old woman's room. It was already quite late. The old woman was asleep. Bylinkin shook her for a long time, but she kept wriggling and kicking, refusing to wake up and understand what was happening.

"Wake up, Ma," Bylinkin said sternly. "Listen, can't Lizochka and I count on the least bit of comfort? Do you expect our underthings to just flutter on the windowsills?"

Once the old woman understood, with great difficulty, what was being asked of her, she began to explain that the chest of drawers had stood in its place for fifty-one years, and that she had no intention of dragging it in all directions, tossing it to the left and to the right, in the fifty-second year of its existence. And it's not like she could make a chest of drawers with her own hands. It was too late, at her age, to learn the craft of carpentry. High time, she said, that Bylinkin understood this and stopped offending an old woman.

Bylinkin commenced shaming Ma, saying that he, who had twice been shelled by heavy artillery on all fronts, had the right to expect a peaceful life.

"Shame on you, Ma!" Bylinkin said. "Begrudging us a chest of drawers! Well, you can't take it with you to the grave. I hope you know that."

"You can't have the chest of drawers!" the old woman said screechily. "You'll get my furniture when I up and die."

"Right, when you up and die!" Bylinkin said indignantly. "That'll be the day . . ."

Seeing that things had taken a serious turn, the old woman began to weep and wail, saying that the last word belonged to her innocent babe, Mishka Rundukov, since Mishka was the only male representative of the Rundukov clan, and so the chest of drawers, by all rights, belonged to him, not to Lizochka.

Roused from his slumber, Mishka Rundukov was decidedly against giving up the chest of drawers.

"Nothin' doing," said Mishka. "They want our chest of drawers but won't shell out more'n ten kopecks. Chests of drawers cost money."

At that point Bylinkin slammed the door shut and stormed off to his room. Bitterly reproaching Lizochka, he told her that he couldn't do without the chest of drawers—that, as a man seasoned in battle, he knew all about life and refused to abandon his ideals.

Lizochka literally darted back and forth between her mother and Bylinkin, begging them to come to some sort of terms, and offering to drag the chest of drawers from one room to another at regular intervals.

Then Bylinkin asked Lizochka to stop darting about, proposing that she go to bed immediately and gather her strength so as to tackle this fateful question in the morning.

Morning was no better. Many bitter and hurtful truths were uttered on all sides.

The angry old woman said with desperate determination that she now saw him, Vasily Vasilyevich Bylinkin, for what he really was—that today he'd take her chest of drawers, and tomorrow he'd make jelly out of her and eat it up with bread. That's the sort of man he was!

Bylinkin shouted that he would file a petition with the police to have the old woman arrested for spreading false and defamatory rumors.

Lizochka, shrieking quietly, dashed from one to the other, begging them to stop hollering, for heaven's sake, and try and sort the matter out calmly.

The old woman said that she was far past the age of hollering, and that she would tell all and sundry, without any sort of hollering, that Bylinkin had dined with them three times and had never bothered, for the sake of courtesy, to offer a bit of compensation for even one of those meals.

Bylinkin grew terribly agitated and declared acidly that, on his many walks with Lizochka, he had bought her no end of lollipops and marshmallows, as well as two bouquets of flowers, but you didn't see him presenting any bills to Ma.

To which Lizochka replied, biting her lip, that he should cut out the brazen lies—there hadn't been any marshmallows, just a few fruit drops and a small bunch of violets, which wasn't worth a kopeck and, moreover, had faded the very next day.

Lizochka walked out of the room in tears, leaving everything to fate.

Bylinkin wanted to hurry after her and apologize for his inaccurate testimony, but then he locked horns with the old woman again, called her the devil's own ma, spit at her, and ran out of the house.

Bylinkin disappeared for two days—no one knows where. When he returned, he stated in an official tone that he no longer considered it possible to stay with the Rundukovs.

Two days later Bylinkin moved to another apartment, at the Ovchinnikovs'. Lizochka defiantly sat those two days out in her room.

The author doesn't know the details of the move, nor does he know what bitter moments Lizochka endured. He doesn't even know whether she endured them. Had Bylinkin felt any hint of regret, or had he done all this with full awareness and determination?

The author knows only that long after the move—indeed, long after his marriage to Marusya Ovchinnikova—Bylinkin kept calling on Lizochka Rundukova. The two of them would sit side by side, shaken by their misfortune, and exchange insignificant words. From time to time, recalling this or that happy episode or event from the past, they would discuss it with sad and pitiful smiles, holding back their tears.

Sometimes Lizochka's mother would come into the room, and then the three of them would bewail their fate together.

Eventually Bylinkin stopped calling on the Rundukovs. From that point on, whenever he'd encounter Lizochka in the street, he'd give her a proper, reserved bow, and then walk on . . .

6

This is how their love came to an end.

Of course, at another time—say, three hundred years from now—their love wouldn't have come to an end. Dear reader, it would have come into lush and extraordinary flower.

But life dictates its own laws.

Concluding his tale, the author wishes to say that, in the process of unfurling this unsophisticated love story and getting somewhat carried away with the experiences of its protagonists, he had completely lost sight of the nightingale, which was mentioned so mysteriously in the title.

The author fears that the honest reader or typesetter, or even the desperate critic, might be unintentionally disappointed at the tale's conclusion.

"What gives?" they'll say. "Where's the nightingale?"

"Why pull the wool over our eyes?" they'll say. "Why entice the reader with such a light-hearted title?"

It would, of course, be ridiculous to start the love story over again. The author won't even try it. He only wishes to fill in some details.

This happened at the very height, at the very pinnacle of their sentimentalism, when Bylinkin and Lizochka would walk past the town limits and wander around in the woods late into the night. On occasion they would stand there for a long time, in perfectly immobile poses, listening to the chirr of the bugs and the singing of the nightingale. And often enough, at these moments, Lizochka would wring her hands and ask:

"Vasya, what do you think that nightingale's singing about?"

To which Vasya Bylinkin would typically reply, in a reserved tone: "Little bastard wants grub."

And only later, after getting somewhat used to the young lady's psychology, did Bylinkin begin to offer more detailed and nebulous responses. He would speculate that the bird was singing about some spectacularly beautiful future life.

The author is of the same opinion: it was singing about a fabulous future life—which will come, say, three hundred years from now, maybe even sooner. Yes, dear reader, let those three hundred years pass like a dream, and then we'll really live it up.

Of course, if we get there and things are just as rotten, then the author consents, with a cold, empty heart, to consider himself a superfluous figure against the background of the ascendant way of life.

And in that case, he might as well jump under a tram.

1926

A MERRY ADVENTURE

1

No, the author simply can't plop down in bed, gay and lighthearted, with a Russian writer's book in his hands.

For his own peace of mind, the author prefers to plop down with a foreign book.

It's true—these foreigners write mighty pleasant stuff. With them it's all luck and happiness. Nothing but success. And their characters are real lookers, walking around in silk dresses and powder-blue underpants. They take baths almost every single day. Brave, cheerful, lying through their teeth. And the endings are, of course, happy. In general, you close the book with joy in your heart, totally at peace.

Even a thing as unstable as weather—why, it's all fine and dandy, from first page to last. The sun's shining. Scads of greenery, loads of air. Always warm. You've got brass bands playing round the clock. I mean, all that stuff just calms the nerves!

Now let's take a look at our precious Russian literature. First off, the weather's a mess. It's either blizzards or storms. You've got the wind blowing in the characters' faces all the time. And they aren't exactly agreeable folks, these characters. Always flinging curses at each other. Badly dressed. Instead of merry, joyous adventures, you get all sorts of troubles and misfortunes, or stuff that just puts you to sleep.

No, the author doesn't agree with this kind of literature. Sure, there might be lots of good and brilliant books in it, and who the hell knows how many profound ideas and various words—but the author just can't find emotional balance and joy in any of it.

I mean, why is it that the French can depict all these excellent, calming aspects of life and we can't? Come on, comrades—for pity's sake! What—is there a shortage of good facts in our life? Are we lacking in light and cheerful adventures? Or are we, in your opinion, low on ravishing heroines?

Come on, dear comrades! It's all right there, if you look close enough. You've got your love. Your happiness. Your success. Ravishing characters. Bright cheerfulness. Family legacies. Baths. Powder-blue underpants. Lottery-Loans that could net you ten thousand rubles. It's all there for the taking.

So why smear our life in print and thicken the black colors? We see enough boring, awful stuff during these transitional days, so why add to it in literature?

No, the author just can't see eye to eye with our highbrow literature! Of course, he himself came to these decisive thoughts only recently.

Up until very recently, the author too had given himself over to the most desperate and melancholy ideas, attempting to resolve the most unthinkable questions. Enough. Basta! That's no road to happiness.

Maybe one really ought to write easily and cheerfully. Maybe one ought to write only about good, happy things—so that the dear paying customer can derive cheerfulness and joy from the written word, not gloom and melancholy.

In the author's opinion, this is indeed the right way forward.

And now, as the author finishes his composition, he comes to the sad conclusion that the whole book has been written the wrong way.

But what can you do? From this point on, the author undertakes to tell only cheerful, merry, and entertaining stories. Going forward, he renounces all his gloomy thoughts and melancholy moods.

Unfortunately, after poring over his memories of all the events and adventures of recent years, the author must admit, with some embarrassment and confusion, that he can't seem to recall an especially merry story. All he can think of is one more or less suitable little tale—and even that tale isn't particularly merry . . . Still, it may draw a quiet chuckle. In any case, it'll do for a start. Who knows? Later, something a bit more fun might turn up.

Yes, the author knows his reader through and through. All he wants for his money, this reader, are some cheerful, happy experiences.

Now, your literary critic, your highfalutin author, your Rabindranath Tagore—he's bound to get all jolly and excited. "See?" he'll say, rubbing his hands. "See there? Just look at that son of a bitch, pandering to the reader like that. Grab 'im and pound his face to a pulp!"

Dear critics, just hold off on the brawling and face-pounding, will ya? Hang fire, fellas. Let a man say his piece. He's not pandering to the reader—he simply writes as he sees fit, for the sake of a cheerful idea and the general good. In any case, the author's worldly wisdom and his many years of experience, as well as the weak state of his health, keep him from entering the critical fray.

And so, after poring over about a dozen and a half stories of every sort, the author has decided to linger on a certain merry, entertaining adventure worthy of the pen of some outstanding French writer.

In this merry adventure, there were many joyous and keen experiences, much cheerfulness and struggle. There were amorous encounters. The weather was autumnal—and not too bad, at that. And the whole tragicomic epic was capped off with a happy ending.

The author doubts he can recall a better story for starters.

Of course, at first glance, the reader won't detect any particular cheerfulness or joy. But you can't have wall-to-wall joy. You know full well you'd be bored stiff with wall-to-wall joy.

And so, the author will try to narrate, in truthful and cheerful tones, a merry adventure that very recently transpired with Sergey Petrovich Petukhov.

2

Sergey Petrovich Petukhov never went to work on Sundays. On these days of rest and cheerful merriment, Sergey Petrovich would get up late—say, around ten, if not closer to eleven. I mean, just imagine!

Today, however, it wasn't even ten when Sergey Petrovich awoke sweetly in his bed, turned onto his other side, and smiled happily at the approaching morning.

His was the smile of a young, healthy organism, as yet unpawed by doctors. His was the smile of a youth who had seen wonderful dreams, bright prospects, and cheerful horizons during the night.

And indeed, that night Sergey Petrovich had had the pleasure of seeing himself as some sort of young, wealthy dandy. He didn't remember exactly what he had witnessed, but some pretty little mugs, prancing little ladies, light, inoffensive conversations, and luminous smiles had woven themselves into his joyous dreams— happy pictures of youth and fortune.

Sergey Petrovich patted his yawning mouth with the palm of his hand and sat up in bed.

A fairly clean nightgown of thin cotton clung tightly to his high chest and strong young shoulders.

Sergey Petrovich sat on the bed for a long time, hugging his knees and contemplating what he had seen in his dream.

And under the sway of this dream, as well as, perhaps, the sun's shining into the room, Sergey Petrovich began to long for an easy and carefree life, or some kind of fun and merry adventure. He wanted, as it were, to continue his fortunate dream.

He wanted to live in a spacious and cheerful room, no less than seven square meters in size. In his mind, he was already covering the room's floor with fluffy Persian carpets and furnishing it with expensive grand and not-so-grand pianos.

Now he saw himself with a beautiful, rather comely maiden on his arm. He pictured them entering a cafe, where he would drink thick cocoa with Viennese rusks, pay for everything with his own money, and then stagger out into the street.

Sergey Petrovich sighed, cast a calm gaze round his unimaginative lodgings, and suddenly jumped out of bed with a sharp movement.

He jumped out of bed, splashed some water on his face under the tin washing jug, combed his tousled head, and began to tie his tie in front of a small pocket mirror he had tacked up on the wall.

He spent quite some time fiddling with his tie, then with his boots, polishing them to the most desperate splendor. It took him just as long to get his hat to sit right. At last, fully dressed, combed, and lightly perfumed with mint drops, he went out into the street.

It was a wonderful, calm morning in the middle of an Indian summer. Scads of greenery and air, and the sun was so bright it nearly blinded Sergey Petrovich for a moment. A brass band blasting away in the distance—some public figure's funeral.

Sergey stood by the house for a while, twirling his walking stick in his hand, and then set off down the avenue with a light dancing step.

Sergey Petukhov was twenty-five years old. He was young and healthy. He had strong, powerful muscles, large, well-turned features, and beautiful gray eyes with lashes and brows to match. The women he passed in the street glanced with obvious pleasure at his bulging figure, his full, round cheeks, and his trousers, which were freshly ironed and not excessively stained. Sergey Petrovich greeted each woman with a screwed-up eye. From time to time he would turn to watch one of them recede down the street, clearly pondering something or other. He walked slowly and breathed deeply. Occasionally he would whistle some cheerful tune. Every once in a while he would stop next to some girl in front of a storefront and look at her sideways, as if appraising and comparing her with the outstanding young ladies he had seen during the night.

Suddenly Sergey turned and followed a certain passing maiden with his eyes.

"Katyusha Chervyakova in the flesh," thought Sergey Petrovich, and, after standing still a little while, took off after her.

Soon he caught up with the maiden, gasping a bit. He wanted to cover her eyes from behind with a cheerful, playful gesture, and then ask, in a false tone: "Who's got you by the eyes?" But suddenly he remembered that his hands weren't especially clean at the moment—that he had spent part of the morning polishing his boots, and that the poisonous, turpentiny odor of blacking could hardly have faded during his five-minute walk. Sergey decided not to go through with his plan. Instead, he merely came up very close to the girl, tugged at her arm, stamped his feet in a jocular fashion, and exclaimed:

"Hey, don't you move!"

The girl, grown deathly pale, shrank back in fright. She must have assumed that some fool was rolling a cart out from a yard, or that some roughneck had some designs on her. But when she saw Sergey Petrovich, she burst out laughing. Holding hands, the two of them guffawed like children. They literally couldn't utter a single word for ten whole minutes, on account of these laughing fits.

Then, having calmed down a bit, he asked her where she was going. When he learned that she was merely out for a stroll, he took her by the hand and dragged her along with him.

Sergey Petrovich had encountered this girl often enough, but he had never thought about her or called her to mind. Now, however—under the sway of his light, cheerful dream and the invigorating weather—Sergey felt a certain yearning, a kind of amorous flutter in his breast.

He took firm hold of her hand and led her triumphantly through the town, as if inviting passersby to gaze upon this continuation of his dream.

Katyusha Chervyakova, who was accustomed to seeing Sergey Petrovich in a rather gloomy humor, his lower lip protruding petulantly, was decidedly perplexed. She didn't know what happy bug had bitten her beau. But, being jolly and joyful by nature, she bolstered his cheerful, playful state of mind. She talked all sorts of nonsense, and he, choking with laughter and youth, grunted like a hog for the whole street to hear.

Youth, beauty, and the wonderful weather had suddenly bound the two into a fine little pair: they both felt the incipient pangs of love, passion, or something to that effect.

And when they were saying their goodbyes at her gate, Sergey Petrovich began to plead excitedly for another meeting, the sooner the better. He told her that his life was passing quickly, without any special experiences or adventures. He said he was extremely lonely. Loneliness was bending him out of shape. He wished to get as close to Katyusha Chervyakova as possible. Would she accompany him to the cinema at the corner of Kirpichny Lane at seven that night? They would go to the first show, where, sitting side by side, they would watch the drama and mull over, to the sound of the music, what they ought to do next—walk around town or drop in somewhere.

After a bit of wavering for the sake of appearances—saying that she needed to hem her mama's sheets, count her linens, or some such—the girl nevertheless consented quickly, fearing that her beau might change his mind about the movies.

They bid each other a very pleasant, simple goodbye and parted. But Sergey stayed at the gate a moment longer, glanced inside, issued a cheerful snap at the dog that had begun barking at him, and went home to breakfast.

And a hearty breakfast it was. Three scrambled eggs with onions and horseradish. A piece of bologna. Butter. Sergey Petrovich's appetite for bread was insatiable. His hostess had failed to take that into account.

"A fine thing, life," Sergey muttered, eating his scrambled eggs.

3

The author himself doesn't know what's most significant, most, so to speak, magnificent in our lives—what, generally speaking, makes existence worthwhile.

Maybe it's service to the fatherland. Maybe it's service to the people and all that sort of tempestuous ideology. Maybe that's it. Yes, that's probably it. But in the private realm, in the everyday scheme of things, there are, apart from these lofty ideas, other, humbler little notions. And it is these, in large part, that make our lives interesting and attractive.

The author doesn't know a thing about these little notions and has no intention of confusing simple, undercultured minds with his own foolish pronouncements on that score. No, the author has no clue as to what's most attractive in our lives.

And yet, on occasion, it seems to the author that, discounting tasks of public significance, love takes center stage. It seems to him that love is the most attractive activity.

I mean, let's say you're walking about town. It's late. Evening time. Streets are empty. And suppose you're really down in the dumps—maybe you lost your shirt in a card game, or maybe it's just a bad case of Weltschmerz.

So you're walking and walking, and everything seems so damned bad, so damned rotten that you're just about ready to hang yourself on the first street lamp you see, if it's lit.

And suddenly—a window. The light in it is red or pink. It's got curtains, too. So now you stand there, staring at this window from afar, and feel all your petty worries and concerns leaving you, and a smile spreads across your face.

And now it all seems like something beautiful and magnificent—the pink light, the little couch in the window, the silly amorous goings-on.

It all seems somehow basic, unshakable—given once and for all.

Ah, reader! Ah, my dear paying customer! Are you familiar with that precious feeling of love, with genuine amorous flutters and heart troubles? Don't you find that to be the most precious, most attractive element in our lives?

The author asserts once again: he himself does not claim this to be the case. No, he decidedly does not. He hopes that there is something even better and more beautiful in life. It's just that, from time to time, he can see nothing higher than love.

The author, unfortunately, hasn't received much love from women. In fact, he can't even recall whether he's had a single kiss in pink lighting. In all likelihood, he hasn't. The young author's youth passed during those turbulent days of revolution, when there wasn't much lighting of any kind, except for the rising sun. People ate oats then. Rough food, that—fit for a horse. It certainly doesn't arouse subtle romantic desires or make you long for a pink lantern.

But none of this depresses the author—none of it weakens his vigorous love of life and his sense that love is, perhaps, a very grand and attractive activity.

Although Sergey Petrovich Petukhov was younger than the author, he had exactly the same thoughts and precisely the same considerations regarding life and love. He had the same understanding of life as the author, who has been schooled by the experience of living.

And on that famous morning, on that clear Sunday, Sergey Petrovich, having enjoyed his hearty breakfast, lolled about on his bed for an hour and a half, indulging in amorous dreams. He was contemplating the amorous adventure upon which he was embarking, repeating in his mind those clever, cheerful, and energetic words he had spoken to the girl earlier that morning. And he was also thinking that love might go a long way toward brightening his boring and lonely life.

Stretching his legs on the back of the bed, Sergey Petrovich impatiently counted the hours remaining until seven o'clock, when he would sit with his young lady at the cinema. There, to the music of the bravura baby grand and the chatter of the projector, he would speak in a quiet and energetic whisper of the unexpected tenderness that had suddenly overcome him.

It had just struck two.

"Almost six hours of waiting," muttered our impatient hero.

But suddenly, jumping out of bed like a shot, he began to pace quickly about the room, muttering curses and kicking at the chairs and stools that stood in the way of his careless steps.

I mean, really. Why lie about like a son of a bitch? One must act quickly.

At the moment Sergey Petrovich was, in a manner of speaking, without money. The salary he had received a week ago was long gone, expended on all kinds of everyday needs and requirements, and now all our hero had in his pocket were four kopecks of copper and one three-kopeck stamp.

Sergey Petrovich had this firmly in mind when he had spoken to the girl about the cinema. But he hadn't wished to roil his own blood at the time, wondering where he would borrow this, in effect, petty amount. He had decided to think it over at home. But now he'd been lolling about on his matrasses for two hours straight, without taking a single step!

Without a jacket, in shirtsleeves, Sergey Petrovich rushed into the room next door. He wanted to borrow the money he needed from his neighbor, with whom he really did maintain sort of friendly relations. But the neighbor said that he simply couldn't lend Sergey Petrovich the money that day. He believed in Sergey Petrovich's good intentions of returning the money, but, unfortunately, he himself only had two rubles left till payday, and he needed them all. On top of that, he generally refrained from giving loans, considering the practice risky and absolutely stupid.

Sergey Petrovich rushed into the kitchen. He begged the landlady to save him from disaster. But the landlady refused, dryly and obdurately, saying that she herself barely made ends meet, and that, unfortunately, she hadn't gotten around to buying a machine on which she could print as many rubles and twenty-kopeck pieces as she wanted.

Severely crestfallen and even a little agitated, Sergey Petrovich trudged back to his room and again lay down on the bed. He began to ponder methodically where he could get his hands on the requisite dough. It was, in effect, a small amount—seventy kopecks at most.

Sergey Petrovich was so anxious to get this money that, for a single moment, he even clearly saw it in his hand—three twenty-kopeck pieces with one ten-kopeck coin.

Trying to think through everything calmly, Sergey Petrovich went from acquaintance to acquaintance in his mind, begging them in the strongest terms to lend him the amount he needed. But suddenly he came to the conclusion that, in reality, he wouldn't manage to borrow the money. Especially before the first of the month.

Then Sergey Petrovich began to ponder other means of wriggling out of this ugly situation. Perhaps he could sell something?

Yes, of course, he would sell something!

Sergey Petrovich quickly rifled through his dresser, his desk, and his trunk. Nothing—absolutely nothing. Worthless rubbish. Couldn't he hawk his last remaining suit? The landlady's dresser and couch? His old boots, maybe—but how much would they fetch?

Here's what he'd do. Yes, Sergey Petrovich would go right out and sell his meat grinder. He'd gotten it from his late mother, and now it just sat there in a basket. I mean, why the hell hadn't he hawked it earlier?

Sergey quickly knelt beside the bed and pulled out a basket full of dusty domestic junk. Brimming with hope, Sergey removed all kinds of things and objects from the basket, evaluating each of them in his mind. But, yet again, all of it was pure rubbish, of no worth whatsoever. A heap of dusty vials, encrusted bottles, powder boxes with rolled-up recipes. Some sort of heavy counterweight pendant from a pull-down lamp, filled with small shot. A rusty door bolt. Two little hooks. A mousetrap. A shoe tree for boots. A piece of a boot shaft. But then, finally, the meat grinder.

Sergey wiped it clean with a handkerchief and lovingly hefted it in his hand, weighing and evaluating it in his mind.

It was a pretty massive, solid meat grinder with a handle. Back in 1919, they'd used it to grind oats.

Sergey blew the last speck of dust off the thing, wrapped it in a newspaper, and, tossing on his coat, ran headlong to the market.

Sunday's trade was in full swing. People were standing and walking around the square, muttering and waving their arms. They were hawking trousers, boots, and griddlecakes fried in sunflower oil. The roar was terrible, the smell acrid.

Sergey pushed his way through the crowd and found a place off to the side, in full view. He unwrapped his precious burden and held it in his palm, handle up, inviting all passersby to glance at the goods.

"Meat grinder," our hero muttered, attempting to speed things along.

Sergey stood there for a fairly long time—but no one approached him. One full-bodied lady did inquire about the price as she walked past. Upon learning that the price was a ruble and a half, she went into such a state of nervous agitation and indescribable rage that she began to scold and reproach Sergey Petrovich for the whole market to hear, calling him a scoundrel and a marauder. In closing, she proclaimed that he, his machine, and his great-grandmother taken together weren't worth more than a ruble and a quarter.

The crowd that had gathered pressed the expansive lady out of the way.

One enterprising young man immediately separated from the crowd, examined the meat grinder, pulled out his wallet, and, slapping it against his palm, said that a ruble and a half was indeed unheard of these days, and that the meat grinder was decidedly not worth that amount. It was in bad shape. Its blade was dull—I mean, look at that godawful blade. But if the meat grinder's owner wished, he could receive twenty kopecks in cash that very minute.

Sergey refused, proudly shaking his head.

He stood there for some time after that, perfectly still. No one approached him. The crowd had thinned out long ago.

Sergey Petrovich's hands were extremely numb and his heart ached.

But then he suddenly glanced at the market clock and flew into total panic. It was already a quarter to four, and he hadn't made a bit of progress.

At that point Sergey decided, without losing any more precious time, to sell the meat grinder to the first willing customer at any price, so that he could immediately dash off somewhere else and secure the rest of the money.

He sold the meat grinder to some shaggy devil for fifteen kopecks.

The shaggy one took his sweet time counting out the coins into Sergey Petrovich's outstretched hand, and the expression on his face was especially offensive. After counting out thirteen kopecks, he declared, "That'll do ya."

Sergey wanted to cuss the miserable customer in the strongest possible terms, but after glancing at the clock again, he sighed and darted home.

It was four o'clock in the afternoon.

4

Clutching the thirteen kopecks in his fist, Sergey rushed home. Along the way, he pondered various plans and possibilities of acquiring the remaining sum. Alas, his head firmly refused to come up with anything. His forehead was covered with sweat, and his temples throbbed feverishly. The thought that he had less than three hours left prevented him from pondering the situation calmly.

Sergey Petrovich came home and cast a melancholy gaze around his room.

He had decided to hawk some basic element of his bedding—the pillow, perhaps, or a blanket. But now he considered the possibility that, after the cinema, the girl might very well want to visit his humble abode. What would he tell her then? I mean, really—how would he explain the missing blanket? Shame and disgrace. After all, curiosity might drive the young lady to inquire about it herself: "Pray tell, Sergey Petrovich," she might say, "where's your blanket?"

At this thought, Sergey Petrovich's heart bled and pounded furiously, and he decisively rejected this unworthy plan.

But suddenly a new happy thought dawned upon his poor head.

His aunt. His own dear aunt. Aunt Natalya Ivanovna Tupitsyna. Sergey Petrovich's own dear aunt. I mean, what was he, a total moron? Why hadn't he thought of her earlier, the hollow-headed idiot?

Sergey Petrovich's whole being was now seized by the joy and cheer that had abandoned him earlier. He launched into some sort of wild African dance, howling and whipping his coat above his head. Tossing the coat onto his shoulders as he flew down the stairs, Sergey Petrovich set off at a good brisk trot to 4 Gazovaya Street, to see his own dear aunt.

Sergey Petrovich saw his aunt fairly infrequently—no more than twice a year, really, on her birthday and Easter. All the same, she was his own dear aunt. She'd understand. By god, she'd understand. She loved Sergey well enough. You could even say she was mad about her nephew. She had even told him that, after her death, he could have the three men's suits that once belonged to her late husband, who had died six years earlier from a perfectly noncommunicable disease—typhoid fever.

Surely his own dear aunt would give him a hand in this sticky situation.

Here, at last, was Gazovaya Street. And here was attractive No. 4—two stories, with tiny little windows.

Sergey raced through the gate into the courtyard. He shot up to the second story without pausing for breath. The next moment he was in the kitchen.

Two old women were bustling about at the stove. These were the landladies—the quarrelsome Belousov sisters. The younger and more venomous of the crones was down on her hands and knees in front of the open oven, taking coals out and smothering them out of sheer miserliness. The other crone, the older Belousov, was wiping dishes with a greasy towel. Some little fellow—perhaps an offshoot of the Belousovs—sat on a stool, shamelessly gobbling down boiled potatoes.

A tremendous number of cockroaches scurried on the wall in front of the stove. A metal clock with weights hung near the window. Its pendulum swung with terrible speed, hoarsely, grindingly beating out the rhythm of the cockroaches' existence.

When Sergey Petrovich entered the kitchen, the women exchanged mysterious glances. They waved their arms at him, as if inviting him to behave more quietly and not spit so much. Droning over each other, they began to report that his aunt, Natalya Ivanovna Tupitsyna, had been seriously ill for two weeks now, and was even, so to speak, at death's door. A doctor had come out to examine her and didn't say anything especially terrible. He just shrugged his shoulders and prescribed some powders. The next day, toward evening, the powders made the sick woman's legs give out and stopped her tongue and stomach from working. If things went on in this way, with god's help, today or tomorrow, old woman Tupitsyna would move on to another, better world. And as her only legitimate heir, Sergey Petrovich would have to arrange all the coffins and graves on his own, because they certainly didn't have time to work selflessly for god-knows-whose benefit.

Upon hearing these words about his status as heir, Sergey Petrovich took heart and immediately raised the topic of money, but the crones, shocked by his behavior, began to reprimand him for his impatience. Now, after the old woman croaks—that's a different matter. But until that happens, he wouldn't get a kopeck out of this house. Sergey Petrovich's heart sank. His last hope had collapsed. He could barely make out what the women were saying. He pushed the sniveling crones aside and slowly, somewhat unsteadily, went down the hall to his aunt's room.

His aunt lay in her bed, perfectly still, breathing hoarsely and heavily. Sergey Petrovich looked around the room, shooting a quick glance at the old woman's yellow face, with its sharp nose and closed eyes. Sergey Petrovich's breath caught, and he tiptoed carefully back to the kitchen.

He didn't pity his dying aunt. At that moment, he wasn't even thinking of her. His only thought was that he certainly wouldn't get any money out of her that day.

Sergey Petrovich stood in the kitchen a full five minutes, almost completely still. A terrible pallor spread over his face.

Out of respect for his unbearable grief, the two old women tried not to move either. They just sighed soundlessly and dabbed at their lips and eyes with the corners of their headscarves. The kitchen was almost completely silent. All one could hear was the rude little fellow, still smacking his lips and gobbling down potatoes, and the kitchen clock, still rhythmically beating out the movement of time.

Then Sergey Petrovich sighed noisily, glanced sidelong at the ticking clock, and froze in complete and utter stupefaction.

It was after five o'clock.

The minute hand was rounding its first quarter.

For the second time that day, Sergey Petrovich's heart bled. He had an ache in his side. His whole head was drenched in sweat, and his throat was dry and coarse.

Suddenly, this draining anxiety gave way to wild, total despair.

Sergey Petrovich was seized by such a profound nervous frenzy that he barely found his way to the stairs. First he stumbled into the closet, then bumbled, twice, into the bathroom, then spooked the little fellow off the stool, aiming to smack him in the mug. At last the old crones, making signs of the cross, helped him to the door.

His arms and legs were in such a tizzy that he barely made it through the courtyard.

It was only out on the street that Sergey Petrovich got some sort of hold of himself. He plodded home, trying to think of nothing. Nevertheless, thoughts of every kind descended upon his head. He attempted to alleviate his predicament with irony.

"There you are, brother Sergey," he muttered. "Screwed."

But irony didn't help.

He came home and dropped into bed, completely exhausted.

"What's the big deal?" Sergey tried to console himself. "So you've got no money! You call that trouble? That ain't trouble—that's chicken shit. Why poison your last drop of blood? I'll just go over there and tell her straight out—I'm broke. Big whoop. Life's full of little stumbling blocks."

But some kind of stubbornness, some stupid desire to get the money no matter what, would let him think of nothing else.

It seemed to him that the whole meaning of life rested on this question. Either he, Sergey Petrovich Petukhov, would acquire this pitiful sum and take the girl out, so that they could spend the evening as all normal people do, merry and carefree—or he'd be forced to acknowledge his own weakness and be thrown over the side of life.

Sergey Petrovich lay perfectly still. Grand fantastic plans and scenes began to take shape in his mind.

For example, he's strolling down the street and finds a wallet. Or he enters a shop, induces panic and fear in the clerks, and absconds with a tidy sum's worth of goods. Or he walks into the State Bank, hustles the employees into the washroom, and makes off with a bag full of ten-kopeck pieces.

After every such fantasy, Sergey would grin hopelessly and rebuke himself for his impractical approach to events.

He begged himself not to worry, but rather to enumerate—methodically, rigorously, in order, without haste, and without indulging in tempting illusions—all possible solutions to his problem.

But suddenly everything around him—the bed, the room, the pillow—became unbearable. Almost at a run, Sergey Petrovich went out into the street.

Muttering and taking big strides, he walked along the avenue.

Without noticing, he stopped at a watch shop and stared for a long time at the round white face of the clock on display in the window.

He stood there for a long time, watching the minute hand move. It moved very slowly, and Sergey Petrovich's throat grew drier with its every movement.

It was six o'clock in the evening.

The minute hand had even made it some distance past twelve.

Sergey Petrovich turned abruptly and walked onward. Passing the State Bank, he gave a wry grin and drummed his fingers on the sign.

And on he went, grinning.

He walked for a long time down this street and that. And then he saw his aunt's house again.

5

After standing in front of his aunt's house for some time, Sergey Petrovich took a decisive step into the courtyard and began to climb the stairs.

His vague thoughts suddenly took distinct shape.

Sure thing. What's the big deal? He'll walk into his aunt's room and just take something. Or maybe he'll wake her and ask for it. He's got no reason to hide anything from her. After all, he's an heir—he has every right. He has the right, for instance, to open a dresser or some night table and take some petty little trifle. What's the big deal? I mean, he could even warn those two dumb crones.

Sergey Petrovich climbed to the second story, went up to the door, and stood there for a couple minutes, gripped by indecision.

Then he gently tugged at the handle. The door was closed.

Sergey Petrovich wanted to shake the handle a bit louder, but suddenly he heard footsteps in the kitchen. Someone was walking toward the door.

Without knowing why, Sergey Petrovich took fright and leaped in one bound onto the steps leading to the attic.

Just then the hook rattled, the door opened, and one of the landladies, the elder Belousov, walked out onto the landing with a bucket full of slops. She didn't notice Sergey Petrovich and began to descend the stairs.

After waiting a bit, Sergey Petrovich quickly and decisively went up to the unlocked door, carefully opened it, and walked into the kitchen.

The kitchen was empty.

Then, tiptoeing gently and quietly, Sergey Petrovich went down the hall and entered his aunt's room. It was dark.

Sergey was seized by an irrational fear bordering on terror. He took three paces toward his aunt's bed and froze, having stepped on the old woman's soft felt slippers. A shudder ran through his body.

Sergey Petrovich was calmed, somewhat, by the regularity of his aunt's quiet breathing, hoarse though it was. He walked right up to the bed, groped about until he found the night table, and came closer.

Suddenly, with a careless movement of his jittery hand, he knocked some sort of vial off the tabletop. Then, close on the vial's heels, a tablespoon crashed to the floor with a terrible clatter. The aunt moved her head slightly and mumbled something.

Sergey Petrovich froze, trying not to breathe.

Footsteps sounded in the next room. Someone's restless, shuffling feet were moving down the hall.

Sergey Petrovich darted about the room. He ran to the window. Then he turned back, threw open the door, and took off down the dark hall. In his haste, he knocked down the younger Belousov crone, leapt over her body, and ran on.

The old woman hollered terribly, and her scream echoed loudly throughout the house.

Sergey Petrovich dashed into the kitchen, put out the light, and rushed out onto the landing.

He wanted to race downstairs in one breath, but suddenly, up from below, came the sound of hurried footsteps. The crone's terrible scream had roused the whole house, if not the whole street.

Now people of some sort were running up the stairs. Sergey darted about on the landing and again, as before, jumped onto the steps leading to the attic. He sat down—nearly fell down—on the steps at the closed attic door, his heart pounding fiercely. There wasn't enough air. With mouth agape, Sergey Petrovich sat and listened in horror to what was happening below.

People of some sort rushed into the apartment. Someone or other was squealing desperately.

And someone else was shouting and weeping through tears.

Then ten people or so raced out of the apartment and rushed downstairs.

After waiting a few minutes—or maybe as long as half an hour—Sergey Petrovich began to descend the stairs. He crossed the courtyard slowly, almost thoughtfully, in a state of complete, icy calm, with his hands behind his back. He encountered no one and found himself out on the street.

There, at the gate, a crowd of people had gathered.

"Well?" someone asked Sergey Petrovich. "D'you get 'im?"

Sergey Petrovich muttered something in response and quietly, somewhat unsteadily, set off for home.

He slunk to his room like a shadow. Then he went into the kitchen and glanced at the landlady's alarm clock.

It was a quarter to nine.

Sergey Petrovich grinned, took off his jacket and trousers, and for a long time paced his room in his underpants. He was trying to determine exactly where he had been at seven o'clock in the evening. He couldn't.

Suddenly the blood rushed to his head. He pictured in his mind the young lady's bewildered face as she had waited for him for an hour or more.

Then Sergey Petrovich grinned again and lay down on the bed. He slept restlessly, frequently muttering in his sleep and shifting his pillow.

6

Sergey Petrovich awoke early. It was seven o'clock in the morning.

He was sitting on his bed in his underwear, wistfully lacing his shoes.

At that moment there was a knock at the door and the younger Belousov crone entered his room.

Sergey Petrovich turned terribly pale and rose to his feet. He was shaking and his teeth were chattering in a tattoo. The old woman waved her hands, announcing that he had nothing to be ashamed of, that he was young enough be her great-grandson, and that she'd seen more than her fair share of men over the years, in a wide variety of underpants.

The old woman sat down on a stool, mournfully blew her nose into her headscarf, and solemnly declared that Sergey's aunt, Natalya Ivanovna Tupitsyna, had died earlier that morning.

At first Sergey Petrovich didn't quite understand what the old woman was talking about. He had expected to hear various hints and suspicions about the previous night's incident, but this was something else entirely.

Then, after waiting a few minutes for the sake of basic decency and shedding a few inconsolable tears over the untimely demise of his aunt, the guest launched into a long and detailed account of the horrors of yesterday's raid.

Sergey Petrovych listened indulgently, but soon began to think about his own affairs.

Of course, thought Sergey, he could go right to Katyusha and explain that his aunt had croaked. It was family circumstances, so to speak, that had kept him from having a nice time last night. He'd had to sit at the bedside of a perishing relative.

He could do that, of course. But yesterday's excitement—all those terrible shocks—had somewhat dulled Sergey Petrovich's desires. He turned his attention back to the old woman's words.

She was still spinning brazen yarns about yesterday's banditry, never suspecting that the man sitting before her had some knowledge of the case. The crone insisted that it was a gang of three men, led by a woman. And apart from these four, there was a fifth—a finger man—a totally beardless little fellow.

Sergey Petrovich, unable to bite his tongue, suggested that the old woman must have been spooked something awful, mistaking the little Belousov offshoot for a finger man and her dear sister for a gang leader.

The old woman responded bitterly that he ought to keep his useless little pronouncements to himself, and that only her resourcefulness and courage had prevented the bandits from making off with the Belousovs' belongings, to say nothing of Sergey Petrovich's.

Here the old woman broached the most pressing and absorbing of subjects. With great delicacy, she began to address Sergey Petrovich's inheritance.

Yes, of course! In all the excitement, Sergey Petrovich had forgotten about his inheritance. How wonderful!

Sergey Petrovich was once again seized by joy and cheer. Once more, bright prospects and happy horizons opened before him. In his mind, he tried on his aunt's suits and vests. In his mind, he strolled down the street in a dandy new jacket, with Katyusha Chervyakova on his arm. In his mind, he haggled with a Tatar, trying to foist off his aunt's useless junk.

Down with gloom! Down with melancholy! Long live cheerful words, cheerful thoughts, and wonderful desires! How good and great it is to be alive in the world. How good it is—what a joy it is— to perceive life as it actually is, and not as it sometimes appears.

Sergey Petrovich felt like a boy of seventeen. He could have whirled off that very minute, sweeping the younger Belousov into a foxtrot, if only it were decent to dance so soon after a relation croaked.

Sergey Petrovich bade the old woman a polite farewell, grandly declaring that he would, without fail, attend the funeral service later that day. He certainly wasn't going to work. No, first he'd make a beeline to Katyusha Chervyakova's place and leave her the saddest of letters with the finest apologies. Then he'd pay his last respects to his relation.

Sergey Petrovich was even a little worried. He was afraid that the old crones might, at the last minute, pocket his inheritance.

He quickly sat down at the table. Drumming his fingers, he began to ponder the text of his letter.

Joy and happiness weighed on his chest and ruined his concentration.

Sergey Petrovich glanced out the window and froze in complete awe. It was a positively lovely morning. The blue sky and tranquil treetops heralded a wonderful day.

"How nice to be alive," Sergey muttered, opening the window. "How nice to breathe the cool morning air. How nice to be in love with some comely young lady."

Sergey Petrovich sat down again, decisively. He offered Katyusha a few words by way of explanation and requested that she meet him without fail, at seven o'clock, at the appointed place. He sealed the envelope, dressed, and went out into the street.

He walked with his head proudly aloft. Yesterday's terror and excitement had drifted off into eternity. Yesterday's minor fear of life had vanished, giving way to vigorous courage.

And really, what's the big deal? Yes, it's true—yesterday, he'd lost a little nerve. He'd been a bit jittery. But nothing had changed. His wonderful life went on as before. And so did his merry amorous adventure. Happiness and good fortune were his constant companions.

Sergey Petrovich handed the letter to the yardman, asking him to pass it on to Katyusha Chervyakova. Then, taking deep breaths of the cool morning air, he set off with a light, prancing step to his former aunt's place.

Sergey arrived just as the funeral service was getting started. The old priest was dragging out his rigmarole, while the Belousov crones were grunting softly, lamenting their last lodger. And yet, at the same time, all this shone with the bright cheerfulness of everyday life.

The late aunt, for her part, was laid out comfortably on a table, atop the best lace pillowcases. Her good-natured face exuded peace and happiness. The old woman looked alive. A certain blush even broke through her yellow skin. It seemed as if she had merely grown tired and lain down on the table for a little shut-eye. She might get up any minute, fully rested, and say, "Here I am, brothers." Sergey Petrovich stared at her for a long time with his kindly eyes.

"Auntie, auntie," he thought. "Brother, what an auntie . . . Finally went and croaked . . ."

Sergey Petrovich stood motionless, his head bowed. He was contemplating the brevity of life and the fragility of the human body, and thinking that it was necessary to cram one's life as full as possible with all sorts of wonderful activities and merry adventures. Nor did these thoughts bring grief and melancholy to his heart—they brought peace and calm.

Without waiting for the end of the service, Sergey Petrovich bowed silently to his motionless aunt and left the room.

He went down the hall to her room. It was neat and tidy. Nothing spoke of death.

Sergey Petrovich cast a hasty glance around the room, sizing everything up. Reaching a tidy little sum—a hundred rubles—he smiled gently, left the room, locked the door, and went out into the street.

He walked down the street, laughing happily. Though it was autumn, the sun—despite all its growing spots—burned him with all its impetuous ardor. There wasn't a hint of wind.

7

That same day, in the evening, Sergey Petrovich met with his little lady.

She showed up a bit later than he did. Worrying and searching for decent words, he took her hands in his and began to explain, right there on the corner, the reasons for his absence the previous night.

Yes, he couldn't get away for a single minute. His aunt had opted to croak in his arms.

He described his aunt's death in strong colors. Then he went on to describe his inheritance.

The maiden blinked her eyelashes prettily and said, with a kind smile, that she had indeed been mighty sore the previous night, but that today she had no complaints.

They sat in the theater, locked in a loving embrace. To the chatter of the projector, Sergey Petrovich whispered all sorts of decent words about his feelings and intentions. The maiden squeezed his hand and leg gratefully, saying that she had taken a shine to his symmetrical appearance at first sight.

After the cinema, Sergey Petrovich and his mademoiselle pounded the pavement for a good long time. And a bit later, she visited his humble abode.

Sergey Petrovich escorted her out of the house at half-past eleven that night. Civilian invalid Zhukov saw the whole thing. He was searching for his cat on the stairs at the time, and he heard Sergey Petrovich say: "If push comes to shove, we'll make it official."

Two weeks later, they made it official.

And six months after that, Sergey Petrovich and his young spouse won fifty rubles on a Peasant Lottery-Loan they had inherited from his former aunt.

Their joy knew no bounds.

1926

LILACS IN BLOOM

1

You can bet they'll take the author to task again for this new work of art.

You can bet they'll accuse him of gross libel against humanity again, of breaking from the masses and so on.

Those little ideas of his, they'll say, aren't so grand.

And his heroes—they're no great shakes either. You'd have a hell of a time finding much social significance in any of them. Their actions ain't likely to arouse, as it were, the burning sympathy of the working masses. No, siree—the working masses won't pledge their unconditional allegiance to such characters.

They've got a point, of course—my characters ain't exactly heavy hitters. They're no leaders, that's for sure. What you've got here is, so to speak, all sorts of insignificant men and women, with their every-day comings, goings, and anxieties. But as for libel against humanity—why, you'll find absolutely nothing of the kind.

Sure, earlier you could take the author to task for—well, if not libel, exactly, then a certain, as it were, surplus of melancholy and a desire to see various dark and coarse sides in nature and humanity.

In his earlier work, the author was indeed fervently mistaken in regard to certain fundamental questions, engaging in downright obscurantism.

Just some two years ago, the author—he didn't like this, he didn't like that. He subjected every little thing to the most desperate criticism and destructive fantasy. Back then—it's embarrassing to admit this before the reader—the author's views had come to such a pass that he began to take offense at the frailty and fragility of the human body, and at the fact that man, for example, consists mainly of water, of moisture.

"Hell's bells, what are we, mushrooms, berries?" the author would exclaim. "Who needs so much water? I mean, really, it's just plain offensive to know what man consists of. Water, chaff, clay, some other extremely mediocre stuff. Coal, I think. And if anything should happen, this whole dusty business starts crawling with germs. I mean, really!" the author would exclaim back in those days, not without chagrin.

Even in such a holy affair as man's external appearance—even in that, the author began to see nothing but coarseness and deficiency.

"Say you come to know a person," the author would muse before his close relatives, "but then you turn away for a minute, or maybe don't see the person for five or six years—well, you're just gobsmacked by the disgusting nature of our external appearance. Take the mouth—some slapdash hole in your mug. Teeth sticking out like a fan. Ears dangling off the sides. The nose is some squiggly bump stuck in the middle, as if on purpose. I tell you, it ain't pretty! No, sir—not much to look at."

That gives you a taste of the sort of foolish and harmful ideas the author had come to back in those days, steeped as he was in the blackest melancholy. The author even subjected so unquestionable and fundamental a thing as the mind to the most desperate criticism.

"Take the mind," the author would muse. "No two ways about it—man has invented lots of curious and entertaining stuff with the mind's help: the microscope, the Gillette razor, the photograph, and so on, and so on. But as for inventing something that would put each and every person on easy street—nothing doing, nothing at all. Meantime, whole centuries fly by, whole eras. The sun's breaking out in spots. Cooling down, you know. I mean, we're in what—year one thousand nine hundred and twenty-nine? Poof! Frittered it all away."

That gives you a taste of the unworthy thoughts that flashed through the author's brain.

But surely they flashed, these thoughts, as a result of the author's illness.

His acute melancholy and irritation with people nearly pushed him over the edge, obscured his horizons, and shut his eyes to a lot of beautiful stuff and to the things currently happening all around us.

And now the author is endlessly glad and pleased that, during those two or three lamentable years, he didn't have occasion to write stories. If he had, great shame would have fallen on his shoulders. Those stories would truly have been malicious slander, crude and boorish libel against the world order and the human way of life.

But now all that melancholy has vanished, and the author again sees everything as it truly is, with his own eyes.

By the way, it's worth noting that, despite his illness, the author never broke from the masses. On the contrary, he lives and ails, so to speak, in the thick of humanity. And he describes events not from the vantage point of Mars, but from our own esteemed Earth, from our own eastern hemisphere, where there happens to be a building that houses a communal apartment in which the author abides and, as it were, observes people personally, just as they are, without any embellishments, guises, or drapery.

And on account of living such a life, the author notices what's what and why. So there's no sense in accusing the author of libeling and insulting people with his words. Especially since the author has, in recent years, developed a particular fondness for people, with all their vices, flaws, and other abovementioned particularities.

Of course, that's the author, but other intellectuals really do utter all sorts of words from time to time. They might say that people are still rubbish. They might say we've got to straighten them out, put them in order. We've got to thrash out the rough elements of their nature. We've got to whip 'em into shape. Only then can life shine in all its marvelous splendor. There's just that one, so to speak, little hurdle. But the author doesn't hold those opinions. He resolutely disavows those views. Oh, sure, we've still got to overcome such unfortunate technical deficiencies as bureaucratism, philistinism, red tape, gang rape, and so on.[1] But everything else, for the time being, is more or less in place and doesn't interfere with the gradual improvement of life.

And if the author were asked: "What do you want? What urgent change, for example, would you make in the people around you, leaving aside the abovementioned deficiencies?"

Well, he'd have plenty trouble coming up with an answer.

No, he doesn't want to change a thing. Except for one little trifle, maybe. I mean greed. I mean the coarse daily grind of material calculation.

I mean, I'd like to see people pay each other visits, you know, for the sake of pleasant heart-to-heart chats, without any hidden motives or calculations. Of course, it's all just a whim, empty fantasy. The author probably has too much time on his hands. But such is his sentimental nature—he'd like to see violets sprouting right on the sidewalk.

2

Of course, it may well be that everything the author has just said bears no direct relation to the work at hand—but people, I'm telling you, he has raised very urgent, pressing questions. And that, you know, is the author's pigheaded nature—he just can't get started with no storytelling before he's had his say.

And yet, in this case, the author's words do indeed, to some extent, bear direct relation to our tale. Especially since he raised the topic of various self-serving calculations. It just so happens that the hero of this tale came face to face with precisely such circumstances. So exhausted was he by the whole whirlwind of ensuing events that, I'm telling you, his jaw dropped.

In the wonderful years of his youth, when all of life seemed but a morning stroll—down a boulevard, say—the author was blind to life's shadowy side. He simply didn't notice it. His eyes were on something else. He saw all sorts of merry little things, various beautiful objects and experiences. He saw flowers growing, buds blossoming, clouds floating, and people loving each other warmly and mutually.

But due to his youth, the foolishness of his character, and the naivety of his vision, the author failed to notice *how* all these things happened—that is, what poked and prodded what.

Later, of course, the author began to pay attention. And suddenly he saw all sorts of things.

Here, say, he sees a gray-haired fellow squeezing another fellow's hand, looking him in the eye, uttering words. Had the author seen the same thing earlier, why, he would've taken heart. "Looky here," he would've thought. "Look how pleasant everyone is, how special, how they love each other, and, in general, how wonderfully life's shaping up."

Well, these days the author sets no store by the hallucinations of his visions. The author is gnawed by doubt. He worries, our author: maybe the gray-bearded fellow's squeezing that there hand and looking into them there eyes so's to shore up his shaky position at work, or to grab a chair at a university and read lectures from said chair on beauty and art?

The author will never forget a certain minor incident that transpired not very long ago. This incident literally cuts the author to the quick without a knife. Imagine a lovely little house. Guests coming and going. Hanging around all day, all night. Playing cards. Gulping down coffee with cream. Treating the young hostess real respectful-like, smooching her hands and everything. Well, of course, one day they come and arrest the master of the house, an engineer.[2] The wife, she takes ill and, of course, damn near starves to death. And not a single bastard comes by to check in on her. No one smooches her hands, that's for sure. Hell, they're all afraid this former acquaintance might cast a shadow over them.

Well, after a while, they let the engineer go—turns out he wasn't especially guilty of anything. And suddenly the guests start showing up again. Of course, by then, the engineer had turned a bit gloomy. He wouldn't always come out to greet the guests, and if he did, he'd look at them with a certain degree of fright and bewilderment.

So tell me—would you call that libel? Would you call that evil fabrication? Not a chance. It's exactly the kind of thing we see every minute of our lives. Time to call it as we see it. Otherwise, everything is, you know, beautiful, swell, sounds dandy. But when push comes to shove, it all goes to hell.

But the author never gives in to despair. Especially since he chances to meet, every five years or so, odd fellows who differ drastically from all other citizens.

This is all theoretical talk, of course; what the author wants to tell you is a true story, drawn from the very source of life.

Still, before he commences describing events, the author would like to share a few more doubts.

The thing is, in the course of the story's plot, you'll find two or three ladies whose portraits are none too complimentary.

The author didn't spare any shades or hues in depicting them, and tried to furnish them with a fresh, lifelike appearance. But the portraits didn't turn out quite as the author had wanted. Consequently, these female figures came out badly—each worse than the other.

Many readers, especially of the fairer sex, might take real offense at these womanly types. They might accuse the author of approaching ladies in the wrong way, of being unwilling to extend the same legitimate rights to women as he does to men. In fact, some of the women in the author's life are already offended: really, they say, your lady types never come out too well.

But don't go scolding the author. He himself can't believe what uninteresting ladies spring from his quill.

It's especially strange since the author has, in all likelihood, encountered, for the most part, rather decent, good-natured, and not very evil ladies all his life.

And in general, the way the author sees it, women are, perhaps, better than men. They are, I don't know—somehow a bit more cordial, gentle, responsive, and pleasant.

On account of these views, the author would never allow himself to insult a woman. And if, on occasion, an ambiguity should arise in his story, you can be sure it's simply a misunderstanding. The author begs you to look the other way and not blow your top over trifles.

As far as the author's concerned, of course, all people are equal.

But if you take, just for kicks, the animal kingdom—well, that's a horse of another color.

There you have differences. Even birds have their differences. The male's always more valuable than the female.

There, for example, a siskin's worth, according to the latest calculations, two rubles, while his mate, in the very same store, goes for maybe fifty kopecks, or forty, or even twenty. But you look at the birds—why, they're two peas in a pod! I mean, you literally can't make out which one's something and which one's nothing.

So you sit these birds in a cage. They chew their seeds, drink their water, hop around on their perches, and so on. But then the siskin, he stops drinking water. He grips his perch tight, fixes his bird gaze on the heights, and commences singing.

And that's what accounts for the expense. That's what runs into money.

You cough up the dough for the singing, for the performance.

But what's considered perfectly decent in the world of birds is out of the question among people. Our men aren't worth any more than our ladies. And what's more, everybody sings—the men, the ladies. So all questions and doubts on the subject disappear.

And besides, all the brutal attacks on women in our tale, all the suspicions about women's self-interest, stem directly from our foremost protagonist—a decidedly mistrustful and sickly man. He had served as a warrant officer in the Tsarist army, and was, furthermore, slightly concussed in the head and battered by the revolution. In 1919 he spent many nights in the reeds, fearing the Communists might arrest him, grab him, and exchange him for one of their own.

And all these fears affected his character in a most regrettable way.

In the '20s he was a nervous and irritable subject. His hands trembled.

I mean, he couldn't even put a glass on the table without smashing it with that trembling little hand of his.

Nevertheless, in the struggle for life, his hands did not tremble.

And for this very reason, he did not perish, but survived with honor.

3

Of course, it isn't all that easy for a person to perish. Which is to say, the author believes it isn't all that easy for a person to starve to death, even in the most extreme conditions. If a person's conscious enough—if they've got hands and a foot and a head on their shoulders—then that person can certainly go the extra mile and scrounge up some sustenance, at least by means of charity.

In this case, things never came to charity, although Volodin was in quite a sticky situation in the first years of the revolution.

What's more, he'd spent many years on the military front. He had completely broken away, so to speak, from life. He didn't know how to do anything particularly useful, except for shooting at targets and people. So he still had no idea what use to put himself to.

And, of course, he had no relatives. Nor did he have an apartment. I mean, he literally had nothing.

All he had was his ma, and she too died during the war. On the occasion of her death, her little apartment passed to another pair of quick hands. And so, upon his return, our former military citizen found himself entirely out of work and, as it were, without a portfolio. What's more, the revolution had knocked him clean out of the saddle, and he found himself, so to speak, off to the side—one could even say as a superfluous and harmful element.

Yet he didn't permit too much panic at this crucial moment in his life. He examined, with his clear eyes, what was what and why. He saw the town. He swept the town with his eaglelike gaze. And what he saw was that life went round and round, in just about the same old manner. People walked up and down the streets. Citizens hurried back and forth. Girls promenaded with parasols.

He looked at what was what, paying close attention to what was poking and prodding the whole affair. What he saw was that the revolution had changed many things, but that things hadn't changed enough for him to succumb to panic.

"Well," he thought, "no cause to jump into a lake. I've just got to come up with something quick. If push comes to shove, I could cart around firewood or some kind of fragile furniture. I could, for example, set myself up in petty trade. Or I could marry, for that matter, not without benefit."

And these thoughts even cheered him up.

"I mean," he thought, "that last option won't be especially beneficial these days, but it could provide, say, room and board, heating, and food."

Of course, he wasn't so incorrigible as to be kept by a woman, but providing first aid at a difficult moment in a man's life is no vice.

Besides, he was young and not very old. A little over thirty.

And although his central nervous system had been rather badly battered by upheavals and everyday worries, he was still a fine figure of a man. What's more, he had a favorable and pleasant appearance. A blond, true, but a manly sort of blond.

In addition, he wore trim Italian sideburns on his cheeks. This made his face even more winning, lending it a demonic, bold quality that forced women to shudder from head to toe, lower their eyes, and quickly pull their skirts down over their knees.

Such were the blessings and benefits at his disposal when he began to win a life for himself.

He arrived in town after completing his military service and temporarily settled in the reception room of his acquaintance's apartment. This acquaintance, the photographer Patrikeyev, had made his apartment available out of the kindness of his heart, but he didn't plan on going entirely unrewarded. He registered part of the living space in Volodin's name and, in addition, expected that his lodger would, out of a sense of lively gratitude, occasionally receive Patrikeyev's visitors—that he would open the door for them and write down their names. But Volodin didn't deliver on these economic hopes; instead he ran around town all day long, who knows where, and on certain nights he'd even ring the hell out of the doorbell himself, throwing the house into complete disquiet and disorganization.

These goings-on made the photographer Patrikeyev terribly sad and undermined his health. On certain nights, he would even leap out of bed in his underpants and curse Volodin to high heaven, calling him a scoundrel, a White officer, and a former piss-poor nobleman.[3]

Still, no more than six months later, Volodin did begin to benefit his patron. Of course, this was toward the end, when he had already moved out of Patrikeyev's apartment and married successfully.

You see, the thing is that even in his most minor years Volodin had had a certain inclination and love for artistic drawing. Even as an absolute baby, he had liked to pencil and paint various drawings and pictures.

And now this artistic talent proved unexpectedly useful.

At first as a joke, but later in earnest, he began to help the photographer Patrikeyev, retouching his pictures and plates.

The young ladies making use of Patrikeyev's services would always demand that their faces be photographed in a decent matter, without the wrinkles, lines, blackheads, and other annoying features, which, unfortunately, accompanied their natural human appearance.

Volodin would obscure these blackheads and pimples with his pencil, deftly decorating the photographed persons with shadows and streaks of light.

In a short while, Volodin proved a great success in this line of work, and even began to earn a bit of money for himself, heartily rejoicing at this turn of events.

4

And having mastered this cunning art, he realized that he had taken a definite position in life, and that it would be quite difficult, even nearly impossible, to knock him out of this position. For that would require the destruction of all photographs, a categorical prohibition of cabinet cards, or the complete absence of photographic paper from the market.

Unfortunately, Volodin's life took this profitable turn only after he had taken a decisive step. You see, he had married a certain female citizen, never supposing that his art would soon give him ample opportunity to stand on his own.

Living at the photographer's and having no particular prospects, he had naturally cast glances at the people around him—and especially, of course, at the ladies and women who might have extended their helping, friendly, and concerned hands.

And he did find such a lady, who responded to the call of a perishing man.

This lady was Margarita Vasilyevna Gopkis, a tenant in the house next door.

She had a whole apartment to herself, living there with her younger sister Lola, who, in turn, was married to a brother of mercy, comrade Sypunov.

These two sisters were still quite young, and both were engaged in sewing shirts, underpants, and other objects for civilian use.

They did this out of necessity. This certainly wasn't the miserable fate they had expected when completing their higher education in a girls' school before the revolution.

After receiving such a decent education, they had, of course, dreamed of living in a dignified manner, of marrying exceptional men or professors who would have stuffed their lives full of luxury, pampering, and nice habits.

Meanwhile, life kept passing. The turbulent years of NEP and revolution didn't allow anyone to look around too long. You couldn't cast your anchor exactly where you wanted it.

And so, bemoaning the vicissitudes of life, the younger sister, Lola, quickly married Sypunov, a rough, unshaven character—a brother of mercy, or rather, a male nurse at the municipal hospital.

While the elder sister, Margarita, wallowed in her grief for too long, sighing about her impossible aspirations. Coming to her senses at the age of thirty, she began to scurry to and fro, hoping to snag some overlooked fellow for a husband.

And our friend Volodin wound up in one of her nets.

He had long dreamed of a more suitable way of life, of family comfort, of a nonreception room, of a boiling samovar, and of all those little things that definitely prettify life and lend a quiet charm to petit bourgeois existence.

And here it all was, his for the taking—plus a stable position and an independent income, which was something on the order of a dowry, undeniably sweetening the deal and adding a certain lively interest.

Of course, if Volodin had struck up this acquaintance a bit later, after he had started making money on his own, he wouldn't have taken the plunge so quickly. Especially since he really didn't like Margarita Gopkis, with that dull, monotonous face of hers.

Volodin liked and was attracted to maidens of a different class— you know, the type with dark little hairs on their upper lips. The funny, bravura kind—quick in their movements, who knew how to dance, swim, dive, and talk all sorts of nonsense. While his Margarita, on account of her profession, was sedentary, and far too modest in her movements and actions.

But the die was cast, and the spring uncoiled without stopping.

And so, whenever he passed the house next door, Volodin would pause near her window and engage her in long conversations, talking about this and that. Standing before her in profile or turned three-fourths and tugging at his sideburns, Volodin would say various roundabout things about a decent life and good fortune. And from these conversations he learned definitively that her room was at his disposal—if, of course, he were to do more than just hint at his intentions.

After quickly assessing the whole affair and appraising his lady with a more attentive and demanding eye, he rushed into the fray with a triumphant cry.

That's how this famous marriage took place.

Volodin moved into the Gopkis apartment, adding to their common pot his humble, lonely pillow and his other paltry goods and chattels.

The photographer Patrikeyev walked Volodin to the Gopkis place, shaking his hand and advising him not to let his newly acquired retouching skills wither on the vine.

Margarita Gopkis waved her hands in vexation, saying that, in all likelihood, Volodin wouldn't need to occupy himself with such a painstaking task.

And so Volodin entered into his new life, believing that he had made a profitable merger, based on exact and accurate calculation.

He rubbed his hands vigorously and patted himself on the back in his mind, saying: "Don't you worry, brother Volodin—seems like life's beginning to smile at you too."

But that smile—well, it wasn't so very good-natured.

5

Needless to say, the life of our Volodin changed for the better. He left the comfortless reception room and got a foothold in a luxurious bedroom, filled with all sorts of whatnots, throw pillows, and figurines.

In addition, having previously subsisted on poor, modest fare— scraps, offal—he got a big upgrade in terms of food. He now tucked into various decent dishes—soups, meats, fish balls, tomatoes, and so on. What's more, once a week he drank cocoa with his entire family, admiring and marveling at the fatty drink, the taste of which he had forgotten in the eight or nine years of his comfortless life in action. But Volodin didn't rely on his lawful wife's support.

He didn't abandon his work in the field of photography, and made major advances, earning not only gratitude but, so to speak, hard cash.

Good fresh food enabled Volodin to throw himself into his work with heightened inspiration. And as he didn't have much luck with his young spouse, he had extra motivation to march off to work. He performed his duties so subtly and artistically that all the photographed faces now appeared perfectly angelic, and their living owners were genuinely taken aback by such a happy surprise. They were ever more eager to get themselves photographed, sparing no money and referring more and more new customers to the atelier.

The photographer Patrikeyev valued his employee tremendously and kept giving him little bonuses whenever customers were especially pleased by his artistic performance.

Now Volodin really felt solid ground beneath his feet and realized that he wouldn't be chased out of his position.

And so he began to gain weight, filling out and putting on a calmly independent air. It's not that he ballooned or anything—just that his body wisely stocked up on fats and vitamins for a rainy day, as a precaution.

Of course, Volodin didn't really enjoy any particular peace and contentment.

After eating his fill, gabbing with his wife on domestic themes, and ordering lunch for tomorrow, he would remain in sad loneliness, genuinely grieving at his lack of particular tender affection for his young spouse—that affection which properly prettifies life and makes every bit of petty bullshit feel like an event and a beautiful detail of happy cohabitation. With these thoughts in his head, Volodin would put on his hat and go out into the street—needless to say, having first shaved, powdered his elegant nose, and trimmed his Italian sideburns.

He would walk the streets and look at the passing women, taking a lively interest in their natures, where they were going, and their little mugs. He would stop and follow them with his eyes, whistling some special tune.

And so time passed without notice. Days, weeks, months went by. Three years slipped away quietly. Volodin's young spouse, Margarita Gopkis, literally couldn't tear her eyes off her remarkable husband.

She slaved away like an elephant, literally without straightening her back, wanting to bring her husband the greatest possible benefit.

Wanting to brighten his existence, she bought all sorts of decent and amusing trifles—fetching neckties, watchstraps, and other household bric-a-brac. But he would gaze at them glumly, grudgingly submitting his cheeks to his concubine's plentiful kisses. Sometimes he would simply snap at her rudely and shoo her away, as if she were some pestering fly.

He began to grieve in the open, to sink into thought, and to curse his life.

"No, life just hasn't panned out," our Volodin would mutter, trying to grasp what mistake he had made in his life and his plans.

6

But in the spring—if memory hasn't betrayed us—of 1925, major events took place in the life of our friend, Nikolay Petrovich Volodin. While courting a sweet little maiden, he fell passionately in love with her—or, to put it plainly, went ass over teakettle—and even began to consider making a radical change in his life. He was now earning a decent salary and could contemplate a new, happier life.

He found this young lass altogether pleasant and charming. In a word, she suited his spiritual needs to a T, possessing precisely the physical appearance of which he had dreamed all his life. She was a slender, poetic individual, with dark hair and eyes that shone like stars. But it was her tiny, small little whiskers that filled Volodin with particular delight and made him ponder his situation more seriously.

However, various family circumstances and dark forebodings of loud scandals, and perhaps even face-poundings, forced him to cool his passions and banish his thoughts.

Just in case, he began to treat his wife even more affably. Whenever he left the house, he'd give her a cock and bull story about needing to rush off to some friend or other, and, patting her on the back, would pronounce various affable and inoffensive words.

And Madame Volodin, knowing full well that something of extraordinary importance was taking place, would blink dumbly, unsure of what to do: should she scream and raise hell, or bide her time, gathering incriminating material and evidence?

Volodin would leave the house, meet with his little moppet, and lead her grandly through the streets, brimming with witty phrases, inspiration, and boisterous, seething life.

The maiden would hang on his arm, chattering about her innocent little affairs. She would say that while many married gentlemen might entertain all sorts of unrealizable fantasies, she, in spite of the total debauchery all around her, had a completely different take on things. Only serious circumstances could incline her to more specific facts. Of course, an excessively strong sense of love might also loosen her principles. Sensing that these words contained an amorous confession, Volodin would drag his lady around with particular energy, muttering various irresponsible thoughts and wishes.

Each evening they would depart for the lake, and there, on the high bank, on a bench, or simply on the grass beneath the lilacs, they would embrace tenderly, experiencing every second of their happiness to the fullest.

It was the month of May, and this wonderful time of year—with its beauty, fresh colors, and light, intoxicating air—inspired them to no end.

The author, unfortunately, lacks major poetic gifts and finds it difficult to wield poetic vocabulary. It truly pains him that he has little aptitude for artistic description and, in general, for literary prose.

If he did, the author would create majestic depictions, describing the fresh feelings of two loving hearts against the marvelous background of a springtime landscape, our natural resources, and fragrant lilacs.

The author admits that he has tried many times over to penetrate the secret of artistic description, that secret which our modern literary giants employ with such enviable ease.

However, the pallor of the author's words and the wishy-washiness of his thoughts have prevented him from delving too deeply into the virginal thicket of Russian literary prose.

But in describing the magical scenes of our friends' assignations, full as they were of poetic trembling and melancholy, the author still cannot resist the temptation to plunge into the sweet, forbidden waters of artistic artistry.

And so the author will lovingly dedicate to our lovers a few lines describing the nighttime panorama.

The author begs experienced artists of the word not to judge his modest exercises too sternly. His is no easy task. It's grueling labor.

And yet the author will still try to plunge into high literary art.

The sea was gurbling . . . All of a sudden, the air was filled with quirling, twirring, slarping. This was the sound of the young man unharnessing his shoulders and harnessing his hand in his side pocket.

The world contained a bench. Suddenly a cigarette entered the picture. This was the young man lighting up and gazing lovingly at his maiden.

The sea was gurbling . . . The grass susurrated ceaselessly. Loam and clay crumbled marvelously beneath the lovers' feet.

The maiden glibbed glintily and squintily, nosing the lilacs.[4] Then the air was again filled with artistic quirling, twirring, slarping. And with its wondrous, indescribable brilliance a spectral analysis suddenly illuminated a hilly terrain . . .

Ah, to hell with it! It won't come out right. The author has the courage to admit that he has no talent for so-called artistic literature. To each his own. The lord god gives one fellow a simple, rough tongue, while another fellow's tongue can turn out all sorts of subtle artistic ritornellos every minute.

But the author never did set his sights on high artistry, and so he turns his rough-hewn tongue back to a description of events.

In short, without encroaching on the art of rhetoric, we'll say that our lovers sat above the lake, holding lengthy and endless conversations about love. From time to time they would sigh, fall silent, and listen to the sea gurble and the vegetation susurrate.

The author is always very shocked to hear people speaking about objects without giving thought to their nature and causes.

Many of our eminent writers, and even our strong satirists, usually write the following words, for example, with the greatest of ease: "The lovers sighed."

But what did they sigh for? How come? Why do lovers develop this definite habit of sighing?

By gum, if you bear the title of writer, well, you've got to explain, elucidate these things for the inexperienced reader. Nothing doing. These writers, they just blurt things out and bid you farewell, moving on to the next topic with criminal negligence.

The author, for his part, will try and stick his nose into this business, which doesn't really concern him. According to the popular theory of a certain German dentist, a sigh is nothing more than a delay. That is, he says, what happens inside your organism, so to speak, is a kind of delay, in his words, some sort of inhibition of some forces or other, which are kept from following straight paths to their destinations, and what you get in the end is a sigh.[5]

If someone sighs, well, that means they've been prevented from fulfilling their desires. And back in the bad old days, when love wasn't especially accessible, lovers had plenty cause to sigh most cruelly. Come to think of it, they still may, from time to time.

Such is the simple and glorious course of our life, and such are the modest, discreet, and heroic workings of our organisms.

But this does not prevent the author from treating many excellent things and desires with love.

And so, our young couple talked and sighed. But in the month of June, when the lilacs were already in bloom over the lake, they began to sigh less and less, and, at last, sighed no longer. Now they sat on the bench, leaning toward each other, happy and enraptured.

The sea was gurbling . . . Loam and clay . . .

Ah, to hell with it . . .

During one of these glorious meetings of the heart, as Volodin sat beside the young lady and rattled off all sorts of poetic comparisons and rhymes, he dropped a rather beautiful phrase, which he had, no doubt, swiped from some anthology, though he insisted otherwise.

Seriously, the author very much doubts that Volodin could have managed to formulate such a fanciful and poetic phrase, worthy of nothing else than the pen of a major literary master of the former era.

As he leaned toward the young lady and the two of them sniffed a branch of lilac, he said: "Lilacs bloom for a week and then fade. As does your love."

The young lady froze in perfect delight, demanding that he repeat those marvelous, musical words over and over again.

And he repeated them all evening, mixing in a few verses by Pushkin—"A bird hopping on a branch"—Blok, and other responsible poets.[6]

7

Upon returning home after that sublime evening, Volodin was greeted with wild shouting, wailing, and harsh words.

The whole Gopkis clan, together with the notorious brother of mercy Sypunov, pounced on Volodin and cursed him out for all he was worth, calling him a crook, a scoundrel, and a skirt-chaser.

Brother of mercy Sypunov literally turned cartwheels around the apartment, hollering that he'd gladly bust a head for the sake of a weak woman, should an ungrateful creature such as Volodin go wandering at night with his tail up, destroying their harmonious family idyll.

Meanwhile, Margarita, sensing impending trouble, squealed, shrill as a whistle. Through her whistling and moaning, she howled that such an ugly, cold-blooded beast should simply be kicked out of the house, and that only love—and, most importantly, her wasted youth—kept her from doing it.

Volodin was struck in an especially unpleasant way by the roaring of the younger sister, Lola, who seemingly had nothing to gain from him. Her roaring only created a disturbing atmosphere and intensified the trouble to the level of a major family scandal.

This crude and uncultured little scene stifled all of Volodin's lofty thoughts. Having returned home overflowing with the most profound and elegant experiences, noble sentiments, and the smell of lilac, he now clutched at his head and silently cursed the rash step he had taken in marrying this unbridled old dame who was ruining his youth. Without raising his voice in response to the scandals and cries, he sent the whole family to hell and locked himself in his room. The next morning, at the crack of dawn, he quietly gathered his wardrobe and little odds and ends, preparing to depart.

When the brother of mercy went off to work, Volodin took all his bundles and left the apartment, ignoring the lamentations and unceasing hysterical fainting fits of his better half.

He came to his photographer, who received him with open arms and genuine joy, assuming that Volodin would now start retouching photographs if not for free, then at least on a more economical basis.

Thrilled by his own deed, Volodin promised various friendly and unpaid services without thinking about his words. He burned with a single desire—to see his moppet as quickly as possible, so as to share with her the new and happy turn of events.

And at two in the afternoon he met with her, as always, by the lake, near the chapel.

Taking his moppet by the hand, he told her the whole tale excitedly, adorning his deed with all sorts of heroic details and minutiae. Yes, he had left his home, breaking those hateful bonds and giving the brother of mercy a good face-pounding.

The news pleased the young lady to the utmost. She proclaimed that he was, at last, a free citizen and finally had the right to call his little chickadee his common-law wife.

And how charming everything would be once they began to live together in the same apartment, under the same roof—with him slaving away like an elephant, without a moment's rest, and her doing chores around the house, sewing, taking out the garbage, and so forth and so on.

Volodin was unpleasantly struck, all of a sudden, by this excessively undisguised desire to have him for a husband, to saddle him, to make him bring home the bacon till the end of his days.

He gazed at the young lady somewhat glumly and said that this was all well and good, but that they still needed to examine all these questions from every side, because he wasn't used to situations where loved ones were made to suffer hardships and privations.

He said it just like that, really, wanting to pull the young lady out of her material calculations and restore her to a more elevated state of mind. He was offended that the young lady would regard him in such practical, self-interested terms.

Then, instantly recalling his own marriage and his calculating schemes, Volodin began to peer at the girl searchingly, wanting to penetrate her mind and heart, to find out whether she now entertained the same thoughts that he had entertained in his day.

It appeared to Volodin that the girl's eyes glowed with greedy calculation, the thought of profit, and the desire to secure her position as quickly as possible.

"And besides, I just don't have the money to get married now," he said. He instantly considered his plan of action, deciding to pass himself off as poor and unemployed.

"Yes," he repeated more firmly, and even, so to speak, solemnly, "I don't have the money, I have no money, and, unfortunately, I cannot provide for you with my work and income."

This, of course, wasn't true; he lived well and was gainfully employed, but he wanted to hear lovely, selfless words from the girl's lips—you know, we'll get by somehow, who's counting, and so on, who needs money when your heart's full of feelings, or something like that.

But Olya Sisyaeva, as if in spite, affected not so much by his protestations as by his tone, began to sniffle and mutter some uncomplicated words, which could most likely be taken for expressions of disappointment and frustrated dreams.

"But how can that be?" she said at last. "Just the other day you spoke in a totally different manner and, on the contrary, made all sorts of plans, but now you say the opposite. How can that be?"

"It's very simple," he said gruffly. "Dear friend, you know, I don't run a government agency. My situation, you know, is too precarious and lonely. Right now, quite possibly, I'm almost out of work. I'm almost in need of a job. I myself don't know how I'll make ends meet down the line. Why, dear friend, I might be forced to walk the streets barefoot, begging for food."

The maiden stared at him with bulging glass eyes, trying with all her might to figure out what was happening.

He, meanwhile, continued talking nonsense, bombarding his lady with images of poverty, discomfort, and a lifetime of deprivation.

Later, before parting, they both tried to take the edge off this rough little scene. Strolling for ten minutes or so, they chatted about entirely unrelated and even poetic things. But their talk was strained. And so they parted—with her surprised and uncomprehending, and him more and more convinced of her subtle calculations and considerations.

Returning to his bare reception room, Volodin lay down on the couch and tried to get to the bottom of the young lady's feelings and desires. "Nicely done," he thought. "Thought she had me on the hook! Bet my poverty talk gave her the shock of a lifetime . . ."

Loves him, does she? He'd just see about that. Might be nothing more than calculation.

And although he was less than fully and definitively convinced of her calculations, he still thought in these terms, wishing to hear, as quickly as possible, her words and assurances to the contrary. True love doesn't end at the sight of poverty and misery. If she really did love him, she'd take his hand and tell him various words—something on the order of, you know, big deal, so what? Your poverty doesn't scare me. We'll work hard, striving for this or that.

He lay on the couch, thinking these thoughts, seized by worry and indecision. Then, suddenly, someone rang at the door. It was brother of mercy Sypunov, who asked Volodin, in a harsh tone, to follow him to a neutral place, out into the yard, so that they could speak freely about all the deeds and actions that had recently occurred.

Worrying and not daring to refuse, Volodin put on his hat and went down into the yard.

The whole Gopkis clan was out there, talking animatedly and working itself up into a fine lather.

Without wasting precious time and words, brother of mercy Sypunov approached Volodin and smashed him with a cobblestone that weighed, by all appearances, more than a pound.

Volodin didn't have time to draw back his head. He just jerked to the side and, in so doing, somewhat softened the blow. Grazing his hat, the cobblestone sliced his ear a bit, as well as the skin of his cheek.

Covering his face with his hands, Volodin rushed back toward the house, pursued by another two or three stones launched by the vigorous hand of the defender of weak women. Volodin flew up the stairs in a jiff and quickly shut the door behind him.

The brother of mercy raced after him and, spurred on by hooliganistic impulses, kicked at the door for a while, inviting Volodin to come out and continue their conversation more calmly, without face-pounding.

Volodin stood behind the door with his hand over his wounded ear and held his breath. His heart pounded desperately. Fear had paralyzed his legs.

After beating on the door a little while longer, the brother of mercy declared that if things went on this way, the whole family would pounce on the scoundrel and splash him with sulfuric acid. Unless, of course, he changed his mind and returned to fulfill his responsibilities.

Battered and shaken, Volodin lay on the couch, thinking that everything had collapsed and gone to ruin.

There was no comfort to be found. Even his love was now in doubt. His affection had been deceived and insulted by crude calculations and considerations.

But then, after thinking it over, Volodin again began to question whether this was really the case.

Well, if it wasn't the case, then he'd go to her straightaway and make sure.

Yes, he would go and tell her everything. He would say that life was coming to a head, that he was pursuing his ideals at great peril to his physical well-being, but, at the same time, she needed to know, once and for all, that he literally had nothing to his name.

He was as good as a beggar, starving and out of work. If she wanted to, she could take the risk of marrying such a fellow. And if she didn't, well, they'd shake hands and go their separate ways, like ships at sea.

He wanted to run to her that very minute and utter the foregoing words, but it was already rather late. He removed his bloodstained jacket, rinsed his torn ear under the tap, wrapped a towel around his head, and lay down to sleep.

He slept badly, tossing, turning, and bellowing so loudly that the photographer was forced, on two separate occasions, to yell Volodin's name in order to stifle his bellows.

8

Well, brother of mercy Sypunov, that rough and uncultured character, actually did manage to get his paws on a bottle of sulfuric acid.

He placed it on the windowsill and gave the two sisters a brief lecture on the benefits of this liquid.

"A small splash can't do any harm," he said to the sisters, acting out both roles in the splashing scene. "No need to go heavy at the eyes, of course, but the nose and other elements can stand a little disturbance. What's more, since the victim's mug is bound to turn red, he'll be a less attractive gentleman, so the girls will stop throwing themselves at him. Then he'll have simply no choice but to return to his stall, like a good little boy. The court, of course, will find various circumstances and assign conditional parole."

Margarita Gopkis stood there moaning, sighing, and wringing her hands, saying that if it was really necessary to splash someone, she'd rather splash the whiskered, swarthy little wench who had ruined her happiness.

However, accepting the notion that they would never get Volodin to return with an unspoiled mien, she moaned again and agreed, saying that, for humanitarian reasons, they should at least dilute the poisonous liquid.

The brother of mercy thundered with his voice and banged the bottle on the windowsill, saying that, now that she'd mentioned it, they might as well splash both the damned bastards, who were plucking on his last nerve and disturbing his temper. And he'd be happy to splash some third bastard, to boot—for example, the swarthy gal's ma. What right did she have to let her daughter run loose like that, knocking about with an occupied man?

As for diluting the liquid, well, that just wouldn't fly. Chemistry is an exact science, requiring a definite composition. He didn't have the book-learning to fool around with scientific formulas.

This whole family scene was shrouded by the sobs of the younger sister, Lola, who foresaw major new commotions.

The author hastens to reassure his dear readers that nothing too terribly serious came of this scene. Things ended if not altogether well, then well enough. But the commotion did cause an enormous fright. And our friend Volodin was made to sup sorrow by the bucketful.

The next day, after shaving his face and powdering his damaged ear, Volodin went out into the street and hurried off to see his moppet.

He walked down the street and gesticulated wildly, talking aloud to himself.

He was thinking up all sorts of tricky questions to ask her, which would reveal the young lady's secret, sordid little game.

She was impoverished, dependent on her ma, wishing to secure her position. But she was sorely mistaken. She should know that he hadn't a kopeck to his name. What she saw is what she'd get. A tie and a pair of trousers. What's more, he was out of work, with no prospects for the future. His photographic business brought him nothing—except for the unbearable expense of pencils and erasers. He only did it out of friendship and courtesy to the photographer Patrikeyev, who had ceded him his couch and reception room.

He would say this to her and see what was what. He walked quickly, noticing no one, hearing nothing.

Suddenly he saw his former spouse, Margarita Gopkis, at the corner, by a vacant lot. She was coming his way.

Volodin turned deathly pale and walked slowly toward Margarita, as if under a spell, never taking his eyes off her.

At a distance of three paces, Margarita quietly shouted something and, with an upward wave of the hand, splashed Volodin with acid.

It was a great distance, and the vial had a narrow neck, so only a few drops landed on Volodin's suit.

Volodin dashed aside, hollering shrilly and slapping his face with his palms, wishing to confirm that his visage was unscathed.

Assured of a successful outcome, he turned around and lunged at Margarita Gopkis, who stood by the fence like a shadow. Volodin grabbed her by the throat and started shaking her, striking her head against the fence and shouting some incoherent phrases.

This all transpired on a deserted back street, down which Volodin was in the habit of walking to meet his moppet.

Nevertheless, people began to gather from other streets, peering curiously, trying to make out the spectacle they were about to see.

But the spectacle was coming to an end. Worried lest he be dragged off to the police station, Volodin stopped shaking his madam and quickly set off for home, without so much as glancing over his shoulder.

He was shocked and agitated. His teeth were chattering in a tattoo.

He returned home almost at a run and locked himself inside the apartment.

Needless to say, he couldn't very well go see his moppet in this state.

He was shivering with fever. His legs trembled and his teeth rattled.

Volodin lay on the couch for a while. Then he began to pace about the room, glancing fearfully through the window and listening closely to every noise.

And he didn't leave the house all day, fearing that the brother of mercy might finish him off in the yard or make a cripple out of him, breaking his arms and ribs.

He spent the day in mortal anguish, eating nothing. He only drank water in mind-boggling amounts, cooling and dousing his inner heat.

And all that night, never once shutting his eyes, he pondered the situation that had taken shape, trying to find some decent and inoffensive way out. And he did find a way out, coming to the conclusion that he needed to reach a truce with his former wife and her guardian angel, comrade Sypunov. He, for his part, would not press charges of attempted murder, while they, in exchange, would not beat him to death.

With that settled, his thoughts leapt to another, no less important front, and he began to contemplate, for the hundredth time, what new, decisive words he would utter to his moppet, so as to ensure that he was getting a real person brimming with selfless affection, not some cunning dame with her practical little tricks. He would stop at nothing to achieve this end, regardless of the difficulties and costs. Yes, he would declare himself unemployed and, at first, work for his photographer on the sly, in order to make sure, once and for all, that the young lady was free of calculations and internal considerations.

Volodin already pictured the scenes in his mind: after turning up his jacket collar and diligently drawing the curtains over the windows, he would retouch photographs in secret, tirelessly, day and night. He saw himself working like this for a whole month, or two months, or even a year, putting all the money aside, without spending a kopeck. Then, when he was finally sure of his moppet, he would lay the pile of money at her feet, begging forgiveness for this deed and trial.

And the young lady, with tears in his eyes, would, quite possibly, push his money away—saying, you know, what's the use, who needs so much money, it spoils relations and such.

And that would mark the start of unclouded happiness, of a marvelous, incomparable life.

Tears of joy showed in Volodin's eyes when he imagined such an outcome. He would revolve on his couch vigorously, making all the springs squeak and wiping his eyes with his shirt sleeve.

But then his mind would return to his troubles—to the face-pounding and all the recent gloomy goings-on.

At those moments he would literally grow cold. Fearing in hindsight for his pristine appearance, he would leap up from the couch and run over to the mirror, seeking to reassure himself as to the safety of his face, or over to his suit, in order to examine the singed fabric.

It was a restless, difficult night. He only got a little sleep toward morning.

And in the morning he set out hastily, gray-faced and bleary-eyed, to arrange his affairs. First he would visit his young lady, so as to proceed, as quickly as possible, with the implementation of his plan. Then he would throw in the towel and enter into negotiations with his dear old relatives.

Stepping out into the stairwell, Volodin began brushing his boots, as was his habit, polishing them with a piece of velvet to a dazzling sheen.

He had already brushed one boot, when suddenly, probably due to the cold of the stairwell, he hiccupped. He hiccupped once, then again, and then, after a few seconds, a few more times.

After clearing his throat and engaging in a brief, stimulating gymnastic exercise, Volodin set about vigorously rubbing his other boot. But since the hiccups refused to go away, he went into the kitchen, took a piece of sugar, and set about sucking it, anticipating that it would be downright awkward to speak to a loved one with such a speech impediment.

And still the hiccups refused to go away. He now hiccupped regularly, like a machine, after definite intervals of time lasting a half-minute each.

Slightly flustered by this new, unexpected obstacle, which hindered him from seeing his loved one, he began to pace about the room, singing cheerful and comic songs at the top of his voice so as not to succumb to his inner anxiety and anguish.

After pacing for about an hour, he sat down on the edge of the couch and suddenly realized, with horror, that his hiccups had not only failed to subside but, on the contrary, had grown thicker and more sonorous; it was only that the intervals between the contractions had increased to nearly two minutes in length.

And during these intervals Volodin sat motionless, almost holding his breath, fearfully awaiting the next throat spasm. And when the hiccup came, he'd leap up, throwing his hands in the air and staring straight ahead with dead, otherworldly eyes, seeing nothing.

Volodin languished in this state until two in the afternoon, then finally divulged his misfortune to his cohabitant, the photographer. The photographer Patrikeyev gave a careless laugh and called the matter a mere trifle and sheer nonsense, which he himself experienced on an almost daily basis. Upon hearing these words, Volodin gathered the remnants of his courage and went off to see his Olya Sisyaeva.

He hiccupped the whole way, shuddering from head to toe and shrugging off any notion of propriety.

To make things worse, just as he approached the young lady's home, he began to hiccup so frequently and vigorously that passersby kept turning around and calling him a braying ass and other insulting words.

After summoning the girl with a knock on her window, Volodin prepared for his decisive explanation—sad to say, having plumb forgotten, on account of his new misfortune, all his cunning questions.

Apologizing for his purely nervous hiccups, which were no doubt caused by a light cold and anemia, Volodin planted an elegant kiss on Olya's hand, hiccupping once or twice during this uncomplicated process.

Thinking that grief had driven him to drink, Olya Sisyaeva blinked her lashes, preparing a severe rebuke. But he, thinking more about his disease, babbled incoherent words to the effect that he was an unemployed individual, who had no capital to his name save this one tie and pair of trousers. And that being the case, Olya should say, straightaway, whether she was willing to marry such a fellow, who was destined to a miserable fate, and with whom she might have to walk the streets of the world, as with a blind man, begging for sustenance. Did she really love him no matter what—or what?

Olya Sisyaeva, blushing slightly, said that it was, unfortunately, rather late to be asking questions of that sort. Especially since she was, as she had learned yesterday, expecting, and so it was rather odd and foolish to expect her to listen to such speeches. A husband was a husband—and his duty was to feed his future family, come what may.

Struck by this new discovery and having received no decisive response to his thoughts and doubts, Volodin, dumfounded, completely lost the thread of his plan and stared at the young lady in amazement, hiccupping from time to time.

Then he grabbed her by the hands and asked her to tell him, at the very least, whether she loved him and was taking this step willingly.

And the girl, smiling prettily, said that, of course, no doubt, she did love him, but that he needed to seek serious medical treatment for his nervous hiccups—she didn't see herself marrying a man with such a strange defect.

And so they bade adieu and parted, with her full of confidence, and with him full of indecision and even despair, because he had failed to determine, once and for all, the young lady's feelings.

9

It was very strange and surprising, but Volodin's hiccups wouldn't go away.

After returning home, he went to bed early, harboring the secret hope that, come morning, all would be well and he would resume his simple, marvelous human life. But upon waking he discovered that his misfortune was still with him. True, he hiccupped more seldom now, about once every three minutes, but hiccup he did, with no sign of relief.

Without rising from the couch, and turning cold at the thought that this malady would linger for the rest of his life, Volodin spent all day and night on his back, only dashing to the kitchen every so often to drink a glass of cold water.

The next morning, after raising his head from the pillow and determining that his hiccups still hadn't gone away, Volodin lost all heart. He stopped resisting nature. Meekly surrendering to fate, he lay like a corpse, his body occasionally shuddering beneath the burden of his nervous hiccups.

The photographer Patrikeyev, disturbed by his tenant's strange condition, took serious fright lest he be saddled with an invalid, who'd just lie there, hiccupping round the clock, thereby scaring off clients and visitors.

Without a word to Volodin, he raced off to that fateful creature, Olya Sisyaeva, in order to invite her to the sufferer's bedside, wishing thereby to absolve himself, as quickly as possible, of any moral and material responsibilities and concerns for the man's care.

He came to her and begged her to go with him, saying that if her boyfriend wasn't exactly on his last legs, he was definitely in a very strange condition. He needed help straightaway.

The maiden, abashed by her fiancé's exceptional disease, couldn't quite express her sadness and anxiety. Nevertheless, she immediately agreed to pay the sick man a visit.

Somewhat flustered by the room's penurious and uncomfortable appearance and by the meagerness of its holdings, the young lady stopped in the doorway, at first unable to work up the courage to approach the sufferer.

Catching sight of the young lady, the sufferer leapt up from the couch, but then lay down again, quickly covering his tattered underthings.

The young lady dragged a stool over to the couch and sat down on it, gazing sadly as her boyfriend was jerked hither and thither by his disease.

News of a man who'd been hiccupping for three days straight had caused a bit of a stir among the local population of nearby houses. And rumors of an amorous drama had intensified people's curiosity. The apartment became the site of a genuine pilgrimage, which no single photographer had the power to stop. Everyone wanted to witness how the bride would treat her fiancé, what she would tell him, and how he, with his hiccups, would respond to her.

And lo and behold, here was our brother of mercy Sypunov, rubbing elbows with the other citizens—though he didn't risk entering the room, so as not to frighten the sufferer.

As both next of kin and a medical worker, he held forth authoritatively, before a crowd of curious onlookers, on the condition of the patient, explaining what was happening and what was what.

Needless to say, he hadn't expected such an outcome. Oh, yes, he had certainly put a fright into the fellow, no doubt about that—but he had been motivated by a sense of justice, and by his bonds of kinship with Margarita Gopkis, who would, after all, be left without a mate in her declining years.

However, all these melancholy scenes of disease had touched him deeply. Moreover, he had total consideration for the feeling of love. And so, needless to say, he'd no longer let anyone lay a finger on his former relative, Nikolay Petrovich Volodin. As for dear Margarita, well, in a pinch, she'd just have to spend her life on her own somehow. The disease, for its part, was most likely a purely nervous ailment resulting from the common cold. Why, in their hospital, all sorts of ailments resulted from the common cold—but don't you worry, many survived.

The photographer Patrikeyev, fearing that he might, in all the hubbub, be robbed of his photographic accessories, raised a cry. He urged the public to disperse, or he would summon the police and put a stop to this disgraceful scene by force.

Upon receiving a directive from the photographer, the brother of mercy commenced pushing and shoving the importunate public, brandishing a tripod and goading the visitors toward the kitchen and the stairs. He asked them cordially to disperse posthaste, without provoking him to take more decisive action.

In view of this disgraceful scene, this crying shame, this full airing of their dirty laundry, mademoiselle Olya Sisyaeva began to prattle, saying that they ought to take the patient to the hospital or, at the very least, summon the municipal doctor, who could amputate the excessive public.

Among the visitors there was, incidentally, one, so to speak, former intellectual, a certain Abramov, who declared that this wasn't a matter for doctors—a doctor would only diddle them out of three rubles and make such a mess of things that they'd never set the sick man right.

Far better, the man suggested, to let him undertake an experiment, which would blast this disease at its root.

This certain Abramov did not bear the title of doctor or scientist, but he had a deep understanding of many questions and loved to cure citizens of all sorts of diseases and sufferings with the help of his home remedies.

He said he had an all too clear picture of the malady. That it amounted to an improper movement of the organism. And that it was necessary to interrupt this movement as quickly as possible. Especially since each organism has, so to speak, its own inertia, and once it gets going, well, good luck stopping it. This, he said, is the cause of almost all our diseases and ailments. And it must, he said, be treated vigorously, with a powerful shock to the organism, followed by another jolt, in reverse—because the organism, he said, worked blindly, not knowing in which direction its wheels were spinning or what its work would produce.

He ordered that the patient be placed in a chair, while he, crudely mocking doctors and medicine, went off to the kitchen, there to begin his scientific preparations.

Aided by the brother of mercy, he drew a bucketful of cold water, then scurried through the door on tiptoes, and, with a sudden shout, dumped the water on the head of the patient, who had been blithely sitting on his chair, understanding little of what was happening.

Suddenly forgetting about his ailment, Volodin looked to be spoiling for a fight. In general, the procedure put him in a violent state—he started driving the public out of the apartment and making moves to pummel his homegrown doctor.

But soon enough Volodin calmed down and, having changed his attire, dozed off with his head on his moppet's knees.

The next morning, he rose in perfect health and, after shaving and putting himself in order, returned to his usual way of life.

The author, of course, is not about to argue that this home remedy had a healing effect. In all likelihood, the disease went away by itself, especially since three to four days is a pretty long duration—although, to be sure, the medical profession has witnessed this particular disease last even longer. So who knows? Perhaps the cool water did indeed have a benign effect on our patient's befuddled brains, thus accelerating the healing process.

10

A few days later Volodin and his moppet made it official, and he moved in to her modest apartment.

Their honeymoon was a quiet affair, very serene.

The brother of mercy's remaining anger gave way to pure graciousness, and he even paid the young people a couple of visits. On one of these occasions he graciously borrowed three rubles, though it must be said he never actually promised to return the money. He did, however, give a solemn promise not to kill or lay a further finger on Volodin under any circumstances.

With regard to his earnings and, in general, his salary, Volodin had to admit that he had detracted from it. Sure, he had fibbed a bit, wishing to test her love. There's nothing offensive about that.

While making his confession, he again begged her to tell him whether she'd known he was lying, or whether she hadn't known and had decided to marry him out of disinterested affection.

The little lady, giggling thoughtfully, assured him of the latter, saying that, at first, she didn't know he was lying and was really afraid he was flat broke. But then she saw clear through his transparent actions. Oh, she didn't object, really—he had a legitimate right to get to the bottom of his future spouse.

Listening to this womanly talk, Volodin cursed himself in his thoughts, calling himself an ass and a muttonhead, because he hadn't managed to check the young lady thoroughly and catch her out.

But then, of course, what choice did he have? Especially since his malignant ailment had done him such an ill turn, robbing him of his will and energy and totally muddling his head. He couldn't have found a fitting solution to his problem in that state. What's more, the young lady had simply outplayed him, trumping him with the ace of her condition. But somehow, some way, everything would come to light on its own in the future.

As for poor Margarita Gopkis, she continued to hold a grudge. One day, upon meeting Volodin out on the street, she refused to respond to his reserved bow, turning her profile sideways.

This minor event nevertheless weighed heavily on Volodin, who had lately begun to wish that life were smooth and sweet in every regard, and that the air were full of fluttering doves.

That day he again grew somewhat anxious, recalling the recent events of his life.

He couldn't sleep all night. He tossed and turned in bed, gazing gloomily, searchingly at his spouse.

The young lady was fast asleep, sniffling and smacking her parted lips.

"It was all calculation," thought Volodin. "Of course, she'd known all along. There's no way she would have married him if he was really broke." In his anguish and anxiety, Volodin got out of bed, paced about the room for a while, then walked over to the window. Pressing his blazing forehead against the glass, he stared out at the dark garden, with its trees swaying in the wind.

Then, worried that the cool night air might trigger his disease again, Volodin hurried back to bed. He lay there for a long time, his eyes open, tracing the pattern on the wallpaper with his finger.

"Oh, there's no doubt—she'd known I was lying," Volodin thought again as he drifted off.

But he rose the next morning, cheerful and calm, and tried not to think of such crude matters any longer. And if these matters did occur to him, he would sigh and dismiss them with a wave of his little hand, resigning himself to the fact that no one ever did anything without self-interest.

1929

NOTES

INTRODUCTION

1. E. B. White, "Some Remarks on Humor" (1941), in *The Second Tree from the Corner* (New York: Harper and Brothers, 1954), 173.
2. M. Ol'shevets, "Obyvatel'skii nabat (O 'Sentimental'nykh povestiakh' M. Zoshchenko," *Izvestiia* (August 14, 1927). Reprinted in *Litso i maska Mikhaila Zoshchenko*, ed. Iurii V. Tomashevskii (Moscow: Olimp, 1994), 148–152.
3. See Gregory Carleton, *The Politics of Reception: Critical Constructions of Mikhail Zoshchenko* (Evanston, IL: Northwestern University Press, 1998), 61–62.
4. For a broad introduction to Soviet culture and society under NEP, see Sheila Fitzpatrick, Alexander Rabinowitch, and Stites, eds., *Russia in the Era of NEP: Explorations in Soviet Society and Culture* (Bloomington: Indiana University Press, 1991).
5. On the Proletarian Culture (Proltkult) movement, see Edward J. Brown, *The Proletarian Episode in Russian Literature, 1928–1932* (New York: Columbia University Press, 1953), James Francis Murphy, *The Proletarian Moment: The Controversy over Leftism in Literature* (Chicago: University of Illinois Press, 1991), and Mark D. Steinberg, *Proletarian Imagination: Self, Modernity, and the Sacred in Russia, 1910–1925* (Ithaca, NY: Cornell University Press, 2002).
6. Mikhail Chumandrin, "Chei pisatel'—Mikhail Zoshchenko?," printed in *Zvezda*, no. 3 (1930), 206–219. Reprinted in *Litso i maska Mikhaila Zoshchenko*, 161–178. Discussed, along with other critical responses, in Carleton, 67–68, and throughout.
7. Chumandrin, in *Litso i maska Mikhaila Zoshchenko*, 172, 178.
8. Zoshchenko, "O sebe," in *Begemotnik: Entsiklopediia "Begemota": Avtobiografii, portrety, sharzhi i izbrannye rasskazy, stikhi i risunki nashikh iumoristov—pisatelei i khudozhnikov* (Leningrad, 1928). Reprinted in *Sobranie sochinenii*, ed. I. N. Sukhikh (Moscow: Vremia, 2008), 105–107. My translation.

9. This was established by Iurii Tomashevskii. See his "Chronological Canvas of the Life and Work of Mikhail Zoshchenko" in *Litso i maska Mikhaila Zoshchenko*, 340; an English translation of this "Chronological Canvas" appears in *Russian Studies in Literature* 33, no. 2 (Spring 1997): 60–92. *Russian Studies in Literature* 33, nos. 1 and 2 (1997) feature a number of valuable articles on Zoshchenko. Tomashevskii (1932–1995) was Secretary of the Commission to Preserve Zoshchenko's Literary Heritage and compiled an indispensable volume of reminiscences, *Vospominaniia o Mikhaile Zoshchenko* (St. Petersburg: Khudozhestvennaia literatura, 1995). Linda Hart Scatton's *Mikhail Zoshchenko: Evolution of a Writer* (Cambridge: Cambridge University Press), originally published in 1993 and revised in 2009, is an excellent English-language resource on the author's life and work. A.B. Murphy's *Mikhail Zoshchenko: A Literary Profile* (Oxford: William A. Meeuws, 1981) was the first book-length study of Zoshchenko in English.

10. Zoshchenko, "A Wonderful Audacity," translated by Rose France, in *1917: Stories and Poems from the Russian Revolution*, edited by Boris Dralyuk (London: Pushkin Press, 2016), 206–208.

11. Zoshchenko, "O sebe."

12. See Hongor Oulanoff, *The Serapion Brothers: Theory and Practice* (The Hague, Mouton, 1966) and *The Serapion Brothers: A Critical Anthology*, ed. Gary Kern and Christopher Collins (Ann Arbor, MI: Ardis, 1975).

13. Zoshchenko, "O sebe, ob ideologii i eshche koe o chem," *Literaturnye Zapiski*, no. 3 (August 1, 1922). Reprinted in *Sobranie sochinenii*, 101–103.

14. For more on Zoshchenko's style, in the context of the Russian literary tradition of *skaz* (intentionally nonstandard, markedly oral prose), see Jeremy Hicks, *Mikhail Zoshchenko and the Poetics of Skaz* (Nottingham, England: Astra, 2000).

15. Zoshchenko, "O sebe, o kritikakh i o svoei rabote," in *Mikhail Zoshchenko. Stat'i i materialy*, ed. B. V. Kazanskii and Iu. N. Tynianov (Leningrad: Academia, 1928), 10. Reprinted in *Sobranie sochinenii*, 108–111.

16. Zoshchenko, "O sebe, o kritikakh."

17. Kolenkorov's very name is indicative of his unsuitability, as well as of his odd ontological status. As Lesley Milne points out, "Kolenkorov's name is derived from the word *kolenkor*, or 'calico,' that plain-coloured cloth used, among other things, for bookbinding. *Kolenkor* features also in the idiom '*Eto sovsem drugoi kolenkor*'—'That's quite another kettle of fish.' Kolenkorov's *Sentimental Tales* are indeed quite a different kettle of fish from the officially propagated literature in a post-revolutionary Russia engaged in its grandiose socio-political experiment," *Zoshchenko and the Ilf-Petrov Partnership: How They Laughed*, Birmingham Slavonic Monographs, no. 35 (Birmingham: Centre for Russian and East European Studies, University of Birmingham, 2003), 44.

18. See Thomas P. Hodge, "Freudian Elements in Zoshchenko's *Pered voskhodom solntsa* (1943)," *Slavonic and East European Review* 67, no. 1 (January 1989): 1–28.

19. As Milne writes, Zoshchenko "applied to be reinstated, but in his case it was argued that 'reinstatement' would mean conceding that the original decision to exclude him had been a mistake. Zoshchenko was, accordingly, not 'reinstated' but only 'admitted' to membership, as if for the first time, on the basis of what he had been able to publish between 1946 and 1953," *Zoshchenko and the Ilf-Petrov Partnership*, 10.
20. White, "Some Remarks on Humor," 174.
21. Alexander Zholkovsky's article on the theatrical dimension of Zoshchenko's art is titled "Mikhail Zoshchenko's Shadow Operas," in *Russian Literature and the Other Arts*, ed. Catriona Kelly and Stephen Lovell (New York: Cambridge University Press, 2000): 119–146. Zholkovsky is one of Zoshchenko's most perceptive critics, who has been able to reconcile, convincingly, his "humorous" and "serious" works; see, for instance, " 'What Is the Author Trying to Say with His Artistic Work?': Rereading Zoshchenko's Oeuvre," *Slavic and East European Journal* 40, no. 3 (1996): 458–474, and *Mikhail Zoshchenko: Poetika nedoveriia*, 2nd ed. (Moscow: Izd-vo LKI, 2007).

PREFACE TO THE SECOND EDITION

1. This is Zoshchenko's homage to his close friend and mentor at the World Literature workshop, the great translator, essayist, and children's poet **Korney Chukovsky** (né, Nikolay Vasilyevich Korneychukov, 1882–1969). In his diary entry for August 23, 1927, Chukovsky wrote: "My one and only consolation at this time is Zoshchenko, who often comes and spends whole days with me. He is very worried about his book *What the Nightingale Sang*. He is outraged by a review, published by some idiot in *Izvestiia* [one of the two official Communist Party newspapers], that treats *Nightingale* as a petit bourgeois encomium to petit bourgeois life. In response to the review he has written a hilarious note to the preface for the second edition, claiming that the author of the book is in fact Kolenkorov, one of his characters. Since he is so worried about the book, he was very happy when I told him that I read it as poetry, that the amalgamation of styles he achieves with such virtuosity does not prevent me from sensing the work's lofty—biblical—lyrical qualities," Kornei Chukovsky, *Diary, 1901–1969*, edited by Victor Erlich, translated by Michael Henry Heim (New Haven, CT: Yale University Press, 2005), 202–203.

PREFACE TO THE FOURTH EDITION

1. The tag **"promoted worker"** alludes to the Soviet phenomenon of "vydvizhenstvo," a concerted effort to promote workers to administrative positions with the help of adult education courses. Kolenkorov, Zoshchenko suggests, should be regarded as someone who has been promoted—hastily and, in all likelihood, prematurely— to the rank of author.

1. APOLLO AND TAMARA

1. The **Fourth Congress of the Communist International (Comintern)** was held in Petrograd and Moscow between November 5 and December 5, 1922.

2. **Lenten sugar** is a candylike dessert for Lent, made by boiling sugar (which is refined without egg whites or animal blood serum) in water and fruit juice. Later, non-Lenten versions of the dessert were made of plain sugar boiled in butter and milk. It was sold in crumbled pink or blue pieces, resembling the Scottish tablet, Dutch borstplaat, and French sucre à la crème.

3. *Persian Lilac (Lilas de Perse)* was a popular perfume invented by Henri Brocard (1839–1900) and produced at the Moscow soap and perfumery factory he had founded in 1864. The factory was nationalized in 1917 and, in 1922, renamed New Dawn (Novaya Zarya).

2. PEOPLE

1. Established in 1921, the **Hero of Labor** award was given to outstanding workers in Moscow and Leningrad; in 1927, it was extended to the whole of the Soviet Union.

2. Russian **populism** ("narodnichestvo") was a socialist movement of the 1860s and 1870s. The populists ("narodniki") were urban intellectuals who believed that the key to reform lay with the peasantry, and so "went out to the people," spreading political propaganda throughout the countryside. Unfortunately, most peasants were not receptive. That, in combination with tsarist repression, splintered and radicalized the movement. It was a radical cell of populists—the People's Will (Narodnaya Volya) group—that assassinated Tsar Alexander II in 1881. Jan **Baudouin de Courtenay** (1845–1929) was an influential Slavic linguist. He was born in Warsaw, in Congress Poland, which was in a "personal union" with the Russian Empire and would, in 1867, be absorbed into the imperial realm. He spent most of his career at Russian universities. In addition to his linguistic work, Baudouin de Courtenay was known as an advocate of national revival and limited autonomy for minority groups under Russian rule. In 1914, he was arrested for publishing a pamphlet espousing his federalist views ("The National and Territorial Aspects of Autonomy") and sentenced to two years' imprisonment at the Peter and Paul Fortress in St. Petersburg. He was released after three months.

3. **Jack London**'s works were enormously popular in the Soviet Union, and more or less ideologically acceptable; Nadezhda Krupskaya read two of Jack London's stories to her husband, Vladimir Lenin, in the days before his death. (Nadezhda K. Krupskaya, *Memories of Lenin*, vol. 1, trans. E. Verney [New York: International Publishers, 1930], 209.)

3. A TERRIBLE NIGHT

1. The **German philosopher** is likely Oswald Spengler (1880–1936), whose *The Decline of the West* (*Der Untergang des Abendlandes*, 1918–1922) was influential in the postwar years. For Spengler, primitive human culture began at the end of the last Ice Age; he deduced that Western civilization, modern culture's final phase, had spent its vital energy and would soon begin to decline.

4. WHAT THE NIGHTINGALE SANG

1. The newspaper *Pravda* (*Truth*) was the official organ of the Communist Party of the Soviet Union until 1991.
2. Jacob **Becker**, who immigrated to St. Petersburg from Bavaria in 1841, became one of the most prominent piano manufacturers in Russia. The Becker firm, which had been the official purveyor to Nicholas II, was nationalized in 1917; their factory was renamed Red October (Krasny Oktyabr).
3. The **Living Church**, or "Renovationism," was a schismatic offshoot of the Russian Orthodox Church, which was founded in 1922 and dissolved in 1946. The Living Church accepted Soviet rule and was infiltrated by the secret police; the moral qualities of its de facto leader, Alexander Ivanovich Vvedensky (1889–1946), were questionable.
4. The **People's Commissariat for Naval Affairs** was established in February 1918. In November 1923, it became part of the People's Commissariat for Military and Naval Affairs, which was subsequently dissolved in March 1934 and replaced by the People's Commissariat of Defense.
5. By "**polka tremblam**," Kolenkorov means "Polka Tremblante" ("tramblan" in Russian). It is a partnered dance, better known as the "schottische," which likely originated in Bohemia.
6. The "**flea waltz**" ("Der Flohwalzer") is a simple composition for piano, often taught to beginners. The "**shimmy**" was a popular dance of the Jazz Age, associated with the Kraków-born American actress and dancer Gilda Gray (née Marianna Michalska, 1901–1959). The last reference is, of course, to Franz Liszt's Hungarian **Rhapsodies**.
7. During the 1920s, "**Americanism**" was synonymous with businesslike efficiency and modern methods of production.

6. LILACS IN BLOOM

1. Zoshchenko ends his catalog of "**deficiencies**" with "chubarovshchina"—a term referring to a notorious incident that occurred on August 21, 1926 in Leningrad's

Chubarov Lane, when an unmarried female worker was raped by twenty-six (some accounts say forty) young male workers, a number of whom were members of the League of Young Communists (Komsomol). The incident, and the term "churbarovshchina," came to symbolize lack of ideological discipline.

2. This is an allusion to the arrests and show trials of technicians accused of sabotaging Soviet industry in the late 1920s and 1930s. The first and most famous of these incidents occurred when fifty-three engineers were arrested in the town of Shakhty and put on trial in 1928. Five of the accused were sentenced to death and another forty-four were imprisoned.

3. **White officer**: Zoshchenko uses the term "zlotopogonnik" (person with gold epaulettes), which at the time referred to officers of the White army.

4. Author's note: The maiden smiled playfully and cheerfully, smelling the lilacs.

5. The **"German dentist"** is, in all likelihood, Freud, and what our author describes is some version of the theory of drives. Freudian analysis was tolerated in Soviet Russia in the 1920s but was officially denounced at the 1930 Congress on Human Behavior in Moscow. See Martin A. Miller, *Freud and the Bolsheviks: Psychoanalysis in Imperial Russia and the Soviet Union* (New Haven, CT: Yale University Press, 1998). Zoshchenko had a lifelong interest in Freud, and his autobiography, *Before Sunrise*, can be read as a work of Freudian self-analysis. See note xviii.

6. **Alexander Pushkin** (1799–1837) is regarded as Russia's greatest literary figure, who presided over the Golden Age of Russian poetry; the years of his birth and death essentially bracketed that period. The Symbolist **Alexander Blok** (1880–1921) occupied a similar position during the Silver Age of Russian poetry, which also lasted roughly from 1880 to the early 1920s. The verse "A bird hopping on a branch," which our author attributes to Pushkin, is not to be found in Pushkin's oeuvre.